Advance praise from the book

Cooperative Village

"I thought I came off pretty well. She noticed my cleavage.
I like that."
–Stanley Plotsky, Cooperator

"If she didn't want me feeding the squirrels, why didn't
she just say so? She had to put me in a book?"
–Frieda [no last name], Cooperator

"Thanks for the mention!"
–Sharon Malhouney-Goodman, Social Worker,
Cooperative Village Senior Center

"It's not this book we worry about. It's the next one."
–Managing Director, Nurses in Neighborhoods NY (NINNY)

And Frances Madeson

"So far she's been a good customer."
–Sal from Ashes to Ashes Crematorium

"Ditto."
–Delivery Guy, Warehouse Wines

"I wish Frances would get a cell phone."
–Josh Dishkin, Founder and President of Dishkin Digital Media

"That bitch funny."
–Loiterer on Columbia Street.

"Her, I could take or leave. But the husband's adorable.
You know who he reminds me of? From Law and Order.
Not Jerry Orbach, the other one, the Italian."
–Rivka-Leah, Co-op Management Office

Cooperative Village

a novel by
Frances Madeson

COOPERATIVE VILLAGE

Frances Madeson

CAROL
MRP/CO.

Carol Music Recording and Publishing Company
New York 2007

Muse Laureate, Kathleen Paton
Editor, Madeleine Beckman
Copy Editor, Adam Dressler
Book Design by Tom Koken
Cover Photo by Joel Raskin

People's Parties from *Court and Spark*
Words and Music by Joni Mitchell
© 1973 (Renewed) Crazy Crow Music.
All Rights Administered by Sony/ATV Music Publishing,
8 Music Square West, Nashville, TN 37203.
All Rights Reserved. Used by Permission of Alfred Publishing Co., Inc.

First Edition
Printed in the United States of America
ISBN 978-0-9792772-0-7
Library of Congress Control Number: 2007900218

For information about permission to reproduce selections from this book, kindly write to Permissions at Carol MRP Co. at P.O. Box 571 Knickerbocker Station, NY, NY 10002-9998.

Visit our Web site: www.carolmrp.com

To Joseph, for walking with me.

Saying laughing and crying
You know it's the same release

JONI MITCHELL—*Court and Spark*

Cooperative Village

1

The Gentle Cycle

I don't usually like to start the day chasing my husband around the apartment, kitchen scissors in hand, but today it simply had to be done—Joseph had a long white thread hanging off the new olive green sports coat I'd just bought him at the Syms Labor Day Event, and I could not, in good conscience, let his sartorial magnificence be so commonly marred. Truth be told, I was full of self-admiration for selecting the jacket in the first place, as the color could not match his eyes more perfectly, and I had a coupon, *and* it was under $110 so there was no sales tax. I rest my case.

He was scooting around at a sprightly pace, especially given the early hour, gathering miscellaneous papers—the *Daily Behavior Report*, his moment-to-moment teaching plans—gulping a freshly brewed cup of Colombian Supremo coffee, the beans ground in the store, because who needs the noise or mess?—which is my job to get up every dawn to perk, to give him a nice sendoff, and I don't mind one bit—and socks, he's always rushing to put on his socks, 100% cotton, because he's a man who's on his feet all day and, I'm not ashamed to say, he sweats.

He was hurrying to board the 6:30 city bus he rides the length of Grand Street to the Delancey/Essex stop of the J-M-Z subway line. From there he catches the M, then transfers to the L to his job in the heart of Bushwick, where he teaches 31 seven-year-old public-school kids to sight-read words from the Dolch list, which is a list of the 220 most common English words. I've gained this knowledge as I'm in the process of making eight sets of flashcards with the Dolch-list words. That's 1,760 flashcards I have to make, another task he's assigned me I don't mind one bit, even though I went to a better undergraduate school and I also have a Master's degree. But he's the captain of our ship now, and when the captain gives an order, the sailor just says "aye-aye, captain," if she knows what's good for her. Even though he teaches second grade, he's strictly first class.

I thought he understood what I, in my own humble way, was trying to accomplish on his behalf, the extra effort I was making, and that he'd be sensible enough to cooperate and stand statue-still while I neatly cut the thread, but he remembered yet another form required by the Chancellor—the class rules sheet: e.g., "keep your hands *and feet* to yourself"—and jerked away from me just as the blades were making contact. I startled, losing my precarious angle and sliced into the waffle of the fabric, replacing the problem of a single stray thread—which I tragically realized I could have simply brushed away with my hand; it wasn't even *attached*—with a square-inch patch of newly, needlessly fraying corduroy. I could've wept, but since it was in the back and he'd never see it, I just said, "There you go," and sent him on his way, silently berating myself for demolishing his brand new sports coat, the VISA bill not even paid.

"It's only Hump Day," he said from the door, filling the frame. He's six feet even and, aside from carrying some extra poundage in the middle, is long, elegant, and mostly toned from a daily yoga practice he began a few years ago. His hair, which he keeps tidily trimmed, is turning ever more from its original dark brown to gray, and for that very reason he no longer sports the ticklish moustache he had when I met him. But his wrinkle-free face, shining round eyes and playful smile give him a lusty, youthful aura and by any standard, in anyone's book, he cuts a fine figure. And because it's true what they say about long-time spouses eventually looking similar to each other, you'd simply have to subtract a few years, inches, and pounds, substitute big brown eyes for green ones and swimming for yoga, then strap on some breasts, jangling silver bangle bracelets, metallic Armani bifocals, and voilà!—you'd have me.

"Well, have a good Hump Day, honey."

"Is there anything going on I can look forward to?" he asked while bending over to pick up the morning's *New York Times* and tossing all but the A section, rubber band and all, back inside on the rug before I could get over to pick it up.

"We have opera tickets this weekend."

"We do?" he asked, brightening. "The Met?"

"City Opera. Donizetti. The short one. We're in the nosebleeds."

"The sound's better up there. Are we going with anyone?"

"Just the two of us."

"Good. Kiss me quick, the bus is going to take off. There's a new driver on the route. Transferred down from Hunts Point. She's a demon—gets her kicks watching us all run for it."

"I hear her revving the engine. You better shake a leg." The kiss tasted of coffee—milky and sweet.

"Lock up," he called back from halfway down the hall.

Sipping my own hot mug of absolutely delicious coffee, I watched him from the kitchen window as he made his way through the morning minyan of mothball-scented alter kockers already congregating at the bus stop, shaking their canes in each other's faces to make an urgent point about something that happened at least thirty years ago. I smiled at how dutifully, if not quite eagerly, he was facing his responsibilities as chief breadwinner. Several months ago I flamed out in my previously lucrative career as a professional doormat in the executive offices of Nurses in Neighborhoods NY, the upstart home-nursing nonprofit that claims: *"We Take the Healing to Your House."* Since then we rely exclusively on his paycheck.

You may more easily recognize my former place of employment by its nickname: NINNY. Inaugurated in 2000, it's the ever-expanding home-care agency with offices in a famously refurbished slaughterhouse in the Meatpacking District. The spread in the *New York Times* featured photos of the giant steel hooks still suspended from the vaulted ceilings in the staff lounge-nee-butchering hall. Was the architect presciently implying that NINNY would likely treat its more talented employees like just so many slabs of dead beef and, short of impaling them, be unable to hold onto them? One wonders. I'd venture a guess, but I may or may not have a confidentiality agreement in place as part of my termination, and therefore, may or may not be allowed to do so.

And while I may be currently unemployed after 25 years of relentless employment, I do not agree with those people—like my older brother Sanford who lives in the Berkeley area and coined the term "flame-out" in an e-mail to me the likes of which I hope none of you ever receive from a family member—who say I am not only unemployed but unemployable. I'm determined to prove them wrong one day soon.

The hot pink disc of the sun was surging upward over the East River as Joseph, unsuspecting of the stubbly blemish on the back of his sports coat, got on the bus. From my window perch I blew him a kiss and thought I really must make amends.

So even though it wasn't my usual laundry day, I decided to deviate from what's become a fairly rigid routine, since everyone has told me how much I need structure now that I'm not working, and, to go the extra mile, to launder his whites so he'd have a nice surprise when he looked in his underwear drawer tomorrow. Besides, I reasoned, I myself could use the inherent lift of the whole laundry experience. Someone in the communal laundry room always compliments me on how white my whites are, giving me the opportunity to explain my system (actually developed by my husband) of washing the whites not once, but twice, the first time with too much soap and bleach, the second time with none at all, to rinse the bleach smell away.

I heaved the laundry cart out of our chaotically crowded hall storage closet and put the detergent and bleach bottles in the bottom before filling it with a canvas bag, itself washable, stuffed with his dirty underwear, proud of my ambition as well as my wifely devotion. Descending from the high floor we live on to the ground floor, where the vast laundry facility's housed, I felt this would be a good step towards restoring my equilibrium, something practical and positive I could accomplish. After all, self-esteem comes from performing esteemable acts, and what could be more esteemable than washing my beloved husband's dirty jockeys?

But, when I reached the laundry room with its 18 washers and 12 dryers, I was unpleasantly surprised by a bad smell. It wasn't mildew or mold, it wasn't trash—though the compactor's not far away, nor is the recycling station, and you wouldn't believe if I told you, which I won't, the filthy refuse some sociopaths think it's acceptable to leave there—but an unfamiliar odor. It seemed to be coming from a corner of the laundry room where the three double-load machines stood, and since I had enough dirty clothes to justify using a double-load machine, I made my way over through a tangle of laundry carts on wheels, knocking them hither and yon with a satisfying crack, like breaking a set of billiard balls, sending them skittering and crashing into each other. I pushed my own upright cart past the folding table and the waiting area with the plastic bucket seats to sniff it out.

When I finally turned the corner, I saw a small, rounded heap on the floor that appeared to be a dead body someone had politely shrouded with an exquisitely stitched coverlet. Why did I assume the body was dead? Why not sleeping? I don't know. I can only say that death has a way of announcing itself and making itself known in any room it's ever in and, maybe because we're human beings and live with the knowledge that we are someday going to die ourselves, maybe because of this, we know it instantly when we see it. The coverlet's edge with the label was turned up, revealing *Neiman Marcus—100% Combed Egyptian Cotton*. I don't usually go in for finder's keepers, but the color was the palest of sky blues and I thought it would be really pretty casually folded on the foot of our bed, so I reached down and picked it up.

You could've knocked me over with a feather—because the dead person was Mrs. Plotsky, my very own elderly neighbor. There are over 300 apartments in our building, which is really three apartment towers in one, so what are the chances? Just last night I'd overheard her and her son's usual evening ritual of family intimacy, him yelling curses at her, her so full of piss and vinegar as she screamed back, and now this.

I won't over-dramatize and say I was in shock to find death in the laundry room, even though it's a place I associate more with renewal than dissolution, but it was a little disturbing. Maybe that's why I went ahead and started doing the laundry, which is what I'd come for, knowing that if my hands were busy, my mind would soon follow and clarity would replace confusion. So often I find if you just put your shoulder to the wheel and start pushing, eventually it'll turn and you'll be on your way to wherever it is you were going, and that's what I did now with Mrs. Plotsky dead on the laundry room floor.

As I was pouring the bleach into the slot at the top of the machine, I thought if it were me on the laundry room floor starting to stink up a common area, I'd be more than a little upset with myself. And since I had extra bleach that I didn't absolutely need for Joseph's underwear, and bleach is an excellent odor fighter, I splashed a little on Mrs. Plotsky, thinking it might help. And it did! So then I thought, if a little bleach helps, a lot would probably lick the whole problem altogether.

The machines are front loading, which I generally find very convenient, but now even more so because it would've been too difficult for me to pick the dead weight of Mrs. Plotsky up off the floor, the dead being as heavy as they are, and I very well might've broken my back trying to load her in the top. But with the ease of front loading, I could unfold her legs into the machine, kind of scoop her tiny little self up, and shove her in. I'm not claiming it was easy, but I pride myself on my physical strength, problem-solving abilities, and a certain can-do attitude that's served me well over the years—well, at least it used to before the, you know, flame-out.

Anyway, I wavered about whether to put the new coverlet in with her, and ultimately decided to spring for the additional $1.25 for a separate load, no bleach at all, just to be on the safe side.

Standing before the machine now fully loaded with

Mrs. Plotsky, I debated what would be the best setting. It was a quandary, because I usually use hot water with bleach, but it didn't feel right in this case; I didn't want to make her any more leathery than she already was. I opted for the gentle cycle in cold water, and tired from my efforts of getting her in the machine, neglected to go back upstairs to get the Downy.

It was such a nice morning, September being a gorgeous month in New York City, and I thought I'd take advantage of the day and walk the two blocks over to the Management Office to let them know about the longtime Cooperator dead in the laundry room. Maybe a security camera was broken? I mean, how long had she been lying there to have started to stink? I wasn't sure what it would be exactly, but it seemed that building management just might have a role to play. Before leaving the laundry room, I double-checked the machine door to make sure the lock was securely fastened as I heard her lace-up orthopedic shoes thumpa-bump-bumping quite a bit in there, which frankly surprised me. I would've thought with all the soap I'd used, the bubbles would've made the cycle gentler.

On the way out, I passed our elevators where the shiva notices are posted with alarming frequency and thought, *someone will be writing one up for Mrs. Plotsky pretty soon.* I wondered if I should order a tray from the Glatt Kosher caterers on Essex Street or if I'd already done enough. I decided to talk it over with my husband first. Maybe a box of rugelach from Gertel's on Hester Street would suffice? After all, on the advice of his doctors, Mrs. Plotsky's son had recently had his stomach stapled, which was why he was recuperating in his mother's apartment in the first place, camped out in a behemoth of a rented hospital bed smack in the middle of the living room—and how could he heal with a tray of cold cuts hanging around the house?

The day was so lovely I almost enjoyed running the gauntlet of ancient neighbors inching their walkers forward on the sidewalk outside the building. I even took a moment to admire the tenacity with which they hauled their decrepit, wasted selves onto the touring coach that would speed them to Atlantic City for an action-packed day of inserting nickels into one-armed bandits.

I especially admired the stooped crones who remained unbowed by concerns of personal vanity and who, like catfish, let the thick white hairs grow on their chins and upper lips for all the world to behold. I was glad we'd chosen this community and hoped that services, such as free bus trips and moderately priced annual luncheons at Kutscher's in the Catskills would still be available as we got older. I'd heard them talking and already knew that "they give you so much at the all-you-can-eat-buffet, they should call it the more-than-you-can-ever-possibly-eat-at-one-sitting buffet," and I looked forward to partaking of it someday. But everything in its time.

Rivka-Leah, the experienced customer service associate in the Management Office, who's probably old enough to retire but cannot relinquish the reins of power, buzzed me in so I could wait my turn while she dealt with several other Cooperators who'd arrived before me.

"What're you completely crazy? I'm not giving you a receipt for your maintenance check. The canceled check will be the receipt. We don't do that."

"But I had a problem one time before when I put the check in the rent box, and you people said you never got it and you charged me a late fee. A late fee! Writing the maintenance check is one of the highlights of my month. Do I look like I would ever be late with such an important check?" The crowd, including me, shook its head as one. No, certainly not.

Seeing the tide turning against her, Rivka-Leah had to think fast. "Mr. Abrahamson, if I do it for you then I have to do it for everyone and before you know it that's all I'm doing, sitting here on my *tuchas* all day long making out receipts for rent checks."

"Fine, then let it be on your head. And these people are my witnesses. Don't charge me no late fees. I got witnesses."

"Fine. *Abi gezundt.* Next!"

While the two other Cooperators in line argued heatedly over who was next, I slipped ahead of them. After all, I had a time constraint. I had to transfer my loads from the washer to the dryers, though I wasn't sure about whether to dry Mrs. Plotsky or not. Maybe on low heat?

"Hi Rivka-Leah. How are you this morning?"

"Thank God. What can I do for you?"

"I'm sad to say my neighbor Mrs. Plotsky died. I found her dead in the laundry room."

"Did she have a parking spot?"

"I don't know. I doubt it. She was well into her nineties."

"This is important," Rivka-Leah was wagging her finger in my face. "'Cause if she had a spot, someone else moves up on the list. Wait a minute, I'll ask my son-in-law. ISH-MA-EL," she screamed into the hall-way, "Plotsky in the Y building. Did she have a parking spot?"

"I told you never to call me that," he screamed back. "What're you kidding? The woman's in diapers, she don't drive no more."

"Maybe a storage room?"

"Since when do I know from storage rooms? Ask Fritzy, if you can find him."

Franklin Delano "Fritzy" Mandelbaum was the new wunderkind on the staff, hired right out of the Cornell School of Hotel Management largely on the strength of his honors thesis entitled, "Don't Flatter Yourself: All Living is Assisted." He'd made a splash from day one, riding his Vespa around the complex, his yarmulke securely bobby-pinned to his fiery red curls, proactively looking for problems to solve *before* they even became problems. He was rarely spotted behind his desk.

"FRIT-ZY, Plotsky in Building Y. Did she have a storage room?"

Luckily, he was in the office downloading tunes to his iPod. His answer was also negative.

"No parking spot, no storage room, why're you bothering me with this? I don't have enough to do? Her *fahkakte* son moved in with her after they stapled his *kishkas*, right?"

"Right."

"Tell him. *Abi gezundt.* Next!"

While it didn't feel great being dismissed by Rivka-Leah like that, I realized she was, as I once had been, a very busy woman who had a lot of demands on her time, and I respected the fact that she had many details to manage. I moved along, taking some comfort in the fact that I'd done the responsible, if not wholly appreciated, thing and had been a good Cooperator. Checking the time, I hurried my steps. I hate it when someone in a rush for a machine takes my load out—especially if it means touching our underwear.

It was a good thing I'd started early, when I'd had the place to myself, since even though every single other washer was now full and going, I had my pick of the still-empty dryers. I wheeled over one of the remarkably stable carts the Co-op so generously provides, placed it directly under the washer, and carefully opened the door. A swollen hand flopped out like a flounder and I jumped a little. Reaching into the dampness, I slid my hands under Mrs. Plotsky's armpits and eased her out torso-first, taking it slowly, since she was now completely waterlogged. Her head lolled back heavily on her neck, exposing veins that were a delicate blue against the white of her throat. It was simultaneously awful and touching how vulnerable she was.

She was never a tall woman, but she appeared to have shrunk an inch or two lengthwise. Bent in half at the waist she easily fit in the cart, sitting more or less upright, one arm crooked like she may or may not have been hailing a taxi to the afterlife. Incredibly, her shoes were on the wrong feet, left shoe on right foot, and I laughed because I hadn't noticed it before, and maybe it's one of those laughs that you laugh so you don't cry, because I found it moving beyond measure that, with her various infirmities at her advanced age, she was still sufficiently energetic and independent to dress herself, or try to, and until the last was getting up each day and putting her shoes on one at a time, albeit mixed-up.

When she was settled in the cart, I checked the machine to make sure there was no debris left inside, and it's a good thing I did because I hadn't realized she was carrying change in her pockets and a couple of coffee-flavored Nips®, which I love, but remembering how much bleach I'd used, resisted unwrapping and popping in my mouth. I collected the quarters, dimes, and nickels, but left the pennies because I haven't taken the time to bend over and pick up a penny, shiny or dull, since I was a little girl. It amounted to a buck seventy-five and I put it in my own jeans pocket to give to Mr. Plotsky later.

Taken out of the wash, Mrs. Plotsky was a lot lumpier than when I'd put her in, and I regretted my thoughtlessness in not removing her enormous glasses first, for they were now irreparably cracked, and could not be donated to the Lighthouse for some other poor woman, blind as a bat, to use. The spin cycle had really taken its toll too, and her stringy gray hair was wound around her head like a sleek turban. Though I'd had my doubts about drying her, it now seemed the only way to fluff her out. So not wanting her hair or, God forbid, fingers to get caught in the dryer's air holes, I put her in the laundered canvas bag before pushing her over and tipping her into the Hercules dryer. I decided to go with permanent press. After all, what could be more permanent than death?

Thinking ahead, I was frankly a little worried about how I was going to get her back upstairs to her apartment when she was dry. The Co-op has a very strict policy about removing laundry carts from the laundry room for non-laundry purposes. But then I remembered how at last year's Annual Meeting, someone had suggested the Co-op purchase those big luggage carts, the brass ones with red carpeting like they have in hotels, so people can unload their cars when they come back from upstate, Florida, or even just the Pathmark. And so they did. The Co-op bought two carts for each of the four buildings and our pair sat parked in the lobby, side-by-side, gleaming like golf carts at a Donald Trump resort, which is to say, they were childishly gaudy. But to use them? The procedure? That I didn't know.

I went to consult with Ernesto, the genial if somewhat lax security guard who, as always, was posted in the lobby at his shipshape console decorated with a vase of fresh flowers delivered weekly (Fritzy's sister-in-law's a florist, but why begrudge him throwing a little business her way and anyway who's going to give him a better price?), and a small American flag flying next to the Puerto Rican one, which I recognized from the annual parade in June, a parade I won't go anywhere near because of the flags on sharp pointy sticks all over the place.

Ernesto gave me his usual professional, "Hola, mami." When I first moved in he used to say "Hola, baby," but I asked my husband to speak to him about that. I'm nobody's baby.

Security monitors were stacked on his desk like the set for *Hollywood Squares* and I instantly became mesmerized by the images—first, Frieda, a woman from the fifth floor who was feeding squirrels in the internal Co-op park in defiance of multiple by-laws and several New York City ordinances to boot, in the process creating a culture of dangerous entitlement amongst the wildlife denizens in our midst. My own husband told me he was in our park trying to eat an onion bialy from Kossars while reading the *Sunday New York Times* (the City section's his favorite) when some brazen squirrel had knocked it right off the park bench, wax paper and all. After that outrage I had approached the woman who feeds them and tried to scare her.

"Frieda, you may not be aware of what can happen, but as a young man, my father was viciously bitten on the hand feeding the squirrels in Poe Park. He had to endure a debilitating series of rabies shots—long painful needles right into the abdomen. And he wasn't doing anything different from what you're doing. All the rest of his life, whenever he even saw a squirrel, he doubled over from the memory."

"Poe Park?" she asked, expertly cracking a fresh roasted shell between her thumb and forefinger. "That's the Bronx."

She had me there.

Another camera was trained on our fitness center, where exercisers in their street clothes were holding on to dear life and both rails of the treadmill. While all agreed that their pace was far from aerobic, I'd overheard heated debates in the gym concerning whether, physiologically speaking, their activity should even be characterized as walking, or a new term, such as "power-creeping" was needed to accurately describe it.

Camera three showed something of a situation brewing near the recycling station. Two elderly Cooperators were arguing about who had dibs on the most recent issue of *The Economist*, which someone had thrown on the recycling pile. One couldn't live long in Cooperative Village without encountering this mentality—Why pay good money when it just ends up in the trash anyway?

"Can you turn on the audio?" I asked Ernesto, who, like me, was riveted.

"Sure, mami."

He flicked a switch and the sound came on.

"Who're you kidding pretending to read *The Economist*? I remember when you thought Wolfowitz was a department store in Rockville Center."

"Maybe you don't remember that luncheon at Noah's Ark Deli? After a single glass of lite beer you admitted that you, Mr. Know It All, thought Milton Friedman was the leader of a *klezmer* band."

Both of them had their hands on the magazine and were pushing and pulling in a tug of war that seemed bound for fisticuffs. But the one who'd erroneously thought the Nobel Prize-winning monetarist was a spirited clarinetist suddenly stopped and, seeing something else in the recycling pile that intrigued him, lunged for it and emerged triumphant, holding the latest issue of *Foreign Affairs* high in the air.

"This is what I really wanted to read anyhow. They've got a profile on Kofi Annan's son, that no-goodnik."

The one who didn't know an IMF from an IGA looked wistful, but didn't put up a fight.

It had been such a fascinating and complex encounter that for a moment I pondered the possibility of applying to the Co-op for employment as a security guard, especially since I was home all day anyway—something else to talk over with my husband when he returned, via two trains and a bus, from instructing his unruly but adorable pupils.

Refocusing on the task at hand, I asked Ernesto about using one of the luggage carts, which I realized, given the options, was a much more dignified conveyance for Mrs. Plotsky, since the Maintenance Department keeps the brass so nice and shiny. He told me I needed to leave an I.D. with him.

"What kind of an I.D.?"

"Most people leave a credit card."

Well, I'm sorry but I wasn't born yesterday, and there was just no way I was going to leave a credit card with Ernesto. I have what can only be termed excellent credit, more than I hope ever to need in ten lifetimes, and I was not about to risk tarnishing that sterling and enduring record. No sir, on my lowest days I could always tell myself, "Hey, cheer up, at least you've got excellent credit."

"How about a library card?" I counter-offered.

"Sure, mami." See what I mean? He really is genial.

"Okay," I thought, now we're getting somewhere. "I'll be right back."

In the elevator, I realized I really should stop by and tell Mr. Plotsky that his mother was dead. That way when I brought her back up, it wouldn't be such a bombshell, but I dreaded the idea of even talking to him. The very first time we'd met, it was because a frantic Mrs. Plotsky banged on our door asking us to come pick her son up off the floor because, dizzy from the Percoset they sent him home from the hospital with, he'd fallen out of bed. My husband and I exchanged glances because we'd felt the boom, wondered what the hell it could be, and felt a little guilty that we hadn't investigated.

So Joseph, who I always say is a saint-in-waiting, agreed, and even though sometimes his back isn't so great, we went to help. Mr. Plotsky, as wide as he is tall, 73 to his mother's 93, was indeed on the floor with his pajama pants down around his ankles, his flaccid penis listing to one side in a ragged nest of white pubic hair, hands folded on his Buddhaesque belly, wide white bandages covering his surgical wound, a waggish expression on his Fallstaffian face. "Nice to meet you folks," he said.

My husband, who was christened in the Catholic Church but now identifies himself as a secular humanist, took it in stride, but I was upset. Why? Because in my whole life the only other time I'd ever seen a grown Jewish man naked and not even trying to cover his privates was in the grainy black-and-white Holocaust films they used to show us in summer camp, the despairing victims being herded into the "showers." Maybe it wasn't exactly Mr. Plotsky's fault, but he and the evil engineers of the Final Solution had become indelibly conflated in my mind. That's what happens when you get involved with neighbors.

Nonetheless, once I start something I try and see it all the way through. As my former boss, the Managing Director at the home-care agency, put it in my annual evaluation, I'm "result oriented." But I learned to take his opinions with a grain of salt; after all, he also wrote an agency-wide memo to the staff, urging them to rent the DVD of *Soylent Green*, even though I'd warned him that expressing enthusiasm for a movie about a future society in which old people are cannibalized to serve the nutritional needs of the young could be viewed, especially given our client base, as heartless and needlessly cruel. But you can't always save people from themselves, and maybe you shouldn't even try.

As it turned out, I was right to be wary of going in to the newly singular Plotsky's, because when I got up there, it was, as is often said, not pretty. The door was cracked open, so after knocking and calling hello, I went inside, not because I'm nosy or, God forbid, intrusive, but to save Mr. Plotsky the trouble of traversing the long hallway, not so easy for a man in his condition. Why should I inconvenience him any more than I already was going to by giving him some sad and possibly shocking news?

It took my eyes a moment to adjust to the half-light. Mr. Plotsky, taking advantage of his mother's absence, had somehow cajoled the woman who delivered Meals on Wheels to Mrs. Plotsky—a kindly middle-aged woman with Down Syndrome everyone refers to as "the lovely retarded woman," who, despite her handicap, had found a wonderful niche for herself in life, delivering hot nutritious meals to shut-ins, a woman who on my more isolated and self-pitying days I sometimes envied—to give him, deviant that he is, a lap dance.

I was naturally appalled, and promptly pushed the off button on the boom box, silencing what sounded like Tovah Feldshuh and Dudu Fisher singing an ecstatic duet of that classic *"Yukel, Wu Iz Mein Yukel?"* This caused the lovely retarded woman to cease her unrhythmic gyrations and the orphan-who-didn't-know-it-yet, Mr. Plotsky, to stop his rhythmic clapping, mid-clap, though his jumping jowls quivered a beat or two more.

"Put your poncho back on," I gently but firmly commanded the lovely retarded woman, and helped her get the hood over her enlarged forehead. "People are waiting for their lunches, dear. Shouldn't you be getting along with your other deliveries?"

"Let her have a little fun," Mr. Plotsky jeered at me. "Can't you see the woman's a born dancer?" I'd never seen him so passionate. "She's got a gift. Always remember, my darling young friend, you've got a gift."

"Shake it, but don't break it!" the lovely retarded woman cheered in her signature monotone.

I walked her to the door and watched her, a little girl in a woman's body, gleefully push the elevator button. I waved and smiled and she blew me a big, fat sloppy kiss and I couldn't help echoing the general consensus: What a truly lovely retarded woman! I let her sweet, affectionate gesture give me the boost I needed to deliver my tough announcement, deciding as I walked slowly back inside to take a Socratic approach.

"Mr. Plotsky," I asked in the most dignified tone I could muster, "where's your mother?"

"I don't know. She said something about doing the laundry," he mumbled, a patina of sweat icing his multi-tiered wedding cake of a face.

"When was that?"

"Last night?" the startled septuagenarian wondered aloud.

I was quiet for a moment so he could hear what he had just said and let it sink in. But he seemed to be waiting for something more, so I *utzed* him along a little down the road to the inevitable conclusion. "Mr. Plotsky, your 93-year-old mother goes down to do laundry and doesn't come back more than 12 hours later. Maybe there's something wrong?"

"What could be wrong? She's made it this far."

"What could be wrong?" I sighed and reminded myself to practice patience, because, after all, you only have one mother. "I'm sorry to be the one to tell you this, but your mother won't be needing her Meals on Wheels today."

"Why, she's going to the Seniors?"

"No."

"What then? She's not hungry?"

"That's right, she's not hungry. She'll never be hungry again," I said definitively, briefly closing my eyes for effect. "I'm so sorry."

Agitated, he started fussing around on his bedside table, looking for something. He found his reading glasses, put them on with trembling fingers, and opened his PocketPal datebook. I held my tongue and didn't ask why, if I don't even need a datebook anymore, a practically bed-restricted misanthrope like him needed with one while recovering from major abdominal surgery? Where's he going anyway? Doctor's appointments maybe? He flipped around, finally settling on a page and let out a grating gasp, and I thought okay, so he wanted to check the date he got the news his mother died, it's a coping mechanism, he's letting it in, little by little, in his own way.

"What? What is it, Mr. Plotsky?" I asked even more gently.

"Her Social Security check's supposed to come day

after tomorrow. As a favor, do you think we could keep this just between us until it clears?"

I thought about his request. Like any average person concerned, some might say obsessed, with issues of mortality, I'd read about the grieving process and knew that people did not always react as one would expect to the death of a loved one. Though his immediate focus on money might be construed by some as craven, and likewise his enlistment of me to help him perpetrate a fraud against the federal government (which after all is like stealing from yourself, since it's our government, of us, by us and for us), I tried to see it from his perspective, and if an extra $1,400 could help him get through this terrible moment a little easier, how could I deprive him of it?

On the other hand, these people were fellow Jews. Mrs. Plotsky was, as am I, a descendant of our matriarchs Sarah, Rachel, and Rebecca, and while it's been a long time since I was familiar with the specifics, I'm pretty sure there were some well-established, maybe even—and I'm guessing here—rigorous rules and regulations already in place regarding death and burial, and now that I considered it, I realized I probably should've checked Deuteronomy before laundering her.

But what trumped all this was the irrefutable fact that I'd already reported Mrs. Plotsky's condition to Rivka-Leah in the Management Office, and while this did not necessarily constitute a paper trail, or even evidence of any kind per se, the toothpaste was already out of the tube, and I told Mr. Plotsky so.

"I don't like to say no, but no it must be. Maybe there's someone you can call to help you with the arrangements—a family member, a social worker if she had one?"

This was somewhat disingenuous on my part, as I knew very well that she had a social worker, because I was the one who sicced the NYC Department of Aging on her in the first place after she had gone down to get the mail in a nightgown so old and worn it was see-through, plus she was barefoot, and let's just say she was badly in need of a pedicure and leave it at that.

"Don't worry about it," he told me, not even looking at me at anymore, which I didn't take personally because I'm well aware of the very human tendency to shoot the messenger.

"All right. I'll be bringing her up in about ten minutes," I said after glancing at my wristwatch, noting that I really needed to hustle to get my library card, give it to Ernesto in exchange for the luggage cart, and rush to make it back to the laundry room if I was going to catch the end of the drying cycle.

Back in my own haven of an apartment, I tried to shake off the disturbing images I'd just seen and to remember when I'd last used my library card and where I'd put it. While I was searching, I noticed a lot of dust under the bed and made a mental note to talk to Arcadia, my not exactly bilingual cleaning woman, about it. You may wonder why, if I was so busy looking for my library card, I was poking around under my bed. But the answer's simple: Whenever I start looking for something I've misplaced, like a library card for instance, I always look under the bed first, just to get it out of the way. That way I don't have that lingering, nagging feeling, that maybe it's under the bed.

After that, I checked my wallet and found it there.

I hurried back down to Ernesto—passing a swarm of Cooperators hovering around the mailman as he tried to do his job—let me tell you that man earns every penny—and handed him my library card.

"Okay, mami, it's all yours."

"Thanks a lot, Ernesto." I backed the luggage cart out and carefully steered around the corner and through the fire door to the back service hallway that leads to the laundry room. The cart wasn't heavy, but it was awkward, especially going through doors and making turns, and I thought this must be what it's like being a bus driver for the MTA, another occupation I'd been considering recently, and decided it probably was not for me after all.

I had a little trouble pushing the luggage cart over the door saddle, which seemed unusually high, and, come to think of it, an unnecessary obstacle to gaining easy access to the laundry room, but I'm sure Fritzy has a good reason, not readily apparent to the average layman, for leaving it that way. In my absence, as if after a sudden downpour, when wild mushrooms, some edible, some fatal if merely touched to the lips, spring up seemingly from nowhere, blanketing the mossy forest floor, the laundry room had become lousy with Cooperators.

"Why's she schlepping the brand new luggage cart in the laundry room?" I heard one of the rarer species of fibrous fungi asking everyone or no one, the presence or absence of another listener in earshot not really being a necessary precondition for constant declaiming and endless rhetorical questioning.

33

"Who knows? Don't pay attention, these new Cooperators have their own way of doing things," answered a woman whose housedress by rights should have been exhibited at the Cooper-Hewitt National Design Museum, extravagantly patterned as it was with electrical household appliances, a Mix-Master over her heart, a coffee percolator riding shotgun at her hip. "Personally, I don't want to use the thing—it's too new. Let it get a little older, then I'll use it."

"It's not like in the old days, when we were a real community," said her friend, whose food-specked glasses I dearly longed to snatch off her face and run full force under hot water. "Let's hope she doesn't spill nothing on it. Fritzy went to a lot of trouble to buy those. His cousin's in the business I heard."

I got over the hump in the nick of time—the vultures were already eyeing my dryer with the coverlet, watching the digital numbers ticking down. Fortunately there were still two minutes to go and I could catch my breath, or so I foolishly thought. With time still on the machine, one of the more aggressive Cooperators made an unprecedented move, a preemptive strike equivalent to the Israelis' destruction of the entire fleet of planes in the Egyptian Air Force on the first morning of the Six Days War, which is why it only lasted six days. She reached for the dryer door.

"What do you think you're doing?" I said, all over her in a flash.

"I'm taking it out."

"You're what? It's not even finished yet."

"It's one item, it's probably dry and I'm taking it out."

"You touch that door handle and you're going to have a big problem, you hear me?" Sometimes in life you've got to take a stand or be trampled upon by hordes of indifferent, calloused feet.

"You can't hog a whole dryer for one item." She looked around to shore up her base, but the others were thinking about it. On the one hand she's lived there longer, so their natural inclination, their primordial instincts told them to align themselves with her, but on the other hand, this new one-item rule she'd concocted wasn't sitting well. Would it apply to their own mattress pads, which, with all the nocturnal pishing that goes on around here, require frequent washing?

Just then the dryer cycle ended and, lucky for her, the whole argument became moot. I took out the coverlet to fold on the table.

"Not like that," one of the buzzards screamed at me. "Line your corners up. What do you want, *meshuggenah* creases every which way?"

I'm not so arrogant that I don't know good advice when I hear it, even if it's unsolicited, so I slowed down to do as instructed. Wait until I take my whites out, I thought, that'll really stir up emotions in the room. But to my disappointment they didn't even notice, because by then they were brawling over whose turn it was for the now-empty dryer. As I folded, I listened to their vehement arguments, some cogent, some simply preposterous, and the thought occurred to me that they didn't actually know whose turn it really was, or if they had known, they'd since forgotten and this argument had no legitimate basis and was just an exercise in sheer will. This was like circuit training for them, a way to keep their stamina up for when they had a real fight on their hands, and I further thought if I paid attention I could learn a lot about survival from these tough old birds.

So now I wasn't sure what to do. Should I put the folded laundry on the luggage cart and lay Mrs. Plotsky on top of it, or vice-versa? My strong preference was to lay her down first and pile the laundry on top of her, which had several advantages. First of all, it wouldn't shmoosh my laundry, which I'd gone to some trouble to fold. Second, it would give her a bit more privacy, a little more coverage than the flimsy canvas bag, so she wouldn't be so exposed as we rolled through the hallways. And last, if there was any decomposition, any leakage, then it would leak on the cart which I could wipe down with a rag, and maybe a little ammonia, which all in all seemed a whole lot easier than doing the laundry all over again, for God's sake.

But what really clinched it was my remembering how my court-ordered therapist had told me, shortly after the flame-out, that one of my issues was that I inappropriately squandered my energy by giving too much of myself to others. Then if my efforts weren't as appreciated as I hoped, I suffered. I also learned in psychotherapy that it's our moment-to-moment choices that bring us happiness or sorrow, and so I decided to put this hard-earned wisdom into practice and put myself first for a change. I laid Mrs. Plotsky down and stacked the laundry neatly, respectfully I might add, on top of her.

Lucky for me, the TV was on, Liza Minelli was a guest on *The View*, and the Greek chorus was gathered, rapt, on the other side of the long room.

"I don't care what they say, she's nothing like her mother. That was a talent."

"Chills she used to give me when she sang."

"And her dancing. She never got the credit she deserved for her dancing. So light on her feet and graceful. She looked like she could float right over the rainbow."

"Somewhere, o-vah the rainbow," one of them started to warble.

"Why she had to marry that *faygeleh* Vincent Minelli, I'll never know."

"What choice did she have? They say Mickey Rooney was a wife beater."

"Ernest Borgnine, too."

"Don't forget Johnny Carson."

Mrs. Plotsky and I slipped out unnoticed. We made it without incident past the storage rooms and janitor's bathroom in the service hallway, through the heavy fire door to the elevator. But then, just as I was lining up the luggage cart for what was essentially a parallel parking maneuver, never my strong suit, a new Cooperator came along with a dog on a leash. The terrier immediately knew something was up and danced around on its dainty toes, excitedly barking and tossing its head and tail around in a frenzy of discovery.

When I moved in four years ago, just after privatization, you simply never saw a dog because Cooperative Village is a "No Dog Community." They make you sign something in the application and then if you're lucky enough, as my husband and I were, to rate a Board interview, the Chairman of the Admissions Committee makes you look him in the eye and swear never to get a dog. And now, here, this woman had a dog, and she wasn't even trying to hide it like some of the craftier Cooperators do.

"Perhaps you're unaware, but this is a No Dog Community," I informed her, not telling her anything she didn't already know.

"Oh please," she said rolling her eyes at the security camera, giving her ponytail a sassy toss.

"Fine, if your conscience permits you to have a dog in a community where you signed a paper, etc., that's for you to decide, but you'll have to wait for the next elevator."

"Oh yeah? Well what've you got there under your laundry?"

"None of your business. It's not a dog, that's all you need to know, so step off, sister."

"Please," she whined. "I can't wait, I really have *to go*." And she crossed one leg in front of the other so pathetically I pitied her her enormous thighs, which I could see through her Juicy Couture sweatpants—which even deeply discounted at Century 21, must have cost her plenty—were already hopelessly dimpled.

Maybe I was a little worn out, weakened from lugging Mrs. Plotsky in and out of the washer and dryer, because even though the woman was a chronic and flagrant violator of the House Rules, I relented and let her and her dog on the elevator, but on one condition.

"Fine—you can board, but you have to pick your dog up and hold it."

"I was going to do that anyway," she said, immediately making kissy-face with the dog, which isn't my favorite thing to look at but in this case seemed sincere enough to be stomachable. In all the excitement, I neglected to push the elevator button, and so I had to ride with them all the way up to the penthouse. As soon as they got off, and the doggie yipped his goodbye, I pushed the button for our floor and reached down in my own show of tentative affection and scratched Mrs. Plotsky a little behind her ears and the back of her scruffy neck. This small, playful gesture brought us to a moment of healing that I was only sorry Mrs. Plotsky wasn't fully around to experience. Nevertheless, I found it affirming to see I could still continue to work things out with people I'm close to, even after they're dead, as long as I'm willing to do the emotional work.

Upstairs, I found Mr. Plotsky's door locked, so I knocked. Naturally, I was somewhat impatient to drop Mrs. Plotsky off, since it was my library card on the line, but it's a long hallway, and he wasn't that mobile before the surgery, so I waited—and waited. Finally, when I couldn't take it anymore, I rapped hard again on the metal door and I heard him in there, hollering, "Go away!"

"Mr. Plotsky, it's me, Frances."

"You heard me, I said go away!"

"Mr. Plotsky, don't be ridiculous. I've got your mother with me."

"So leave her out there."

"You know I can't do that." He grew up here, so he knows far better than I that there's a prohibition against leaving any personal items in the hallways, even wet umbrellas. He must be in shock, I thought, overwhelmed by grief. "I'll take her with me for a while until you calm down."

"Suit yourself. I'm not opening the door for you ever again."

"Then I'll huff and I'll puff and I'll blow your house down," I said, perhaps a bit smugly, but I wanted to mirror for him how childish he was being.

"Go fuck yourself, you interfering busybody."

Isn't that rich? And isn't it just like they always say, "No good deed goes unpunished?" But I wasn't going to stand out in the hall and argue with a crazy man, so I wheeled her in to my beautiful one-bedroom apartment with river views in every room and put the kettle on.

"Don't get comfortable," I told her. "We're not staying long." And although my tone was not unkind, it wasn't kind either, and I thought when Mrs. Plotsky was alive, to perform a *mitzvah*, or even just to be neighborly, why couldn't I have invited her in for a single cup of tea and a few Lorna Doones, one time at least, to bring some comfort to an old woman with no daughters to care for her? And then I remembered why: Because I didn't want her on my furniture, which is just as true now as it was then, even more so, since there's no telling what got churned up.

Just then, my computer speakers sent out a little ding, the signal for an incoming e-mail, an all-too infrequent occurrence these days, and I crossed the room with peppy steps in eager anticipation of receiving word from someone, anyone, with my e-mail address. It was from the New York Public Library, letting me know I had an overdue book. Even though my unblemished record as a library borrower is almost as important to my sense of self as my credit rating, I didn't panic, because with the click of the mouse I could renew it and stop the fine from accruing. However, without my bar code, which is on my library card, which Ernesto was now holding, I was powerless. Well doesn't that just beat the band? And I started to fume. Now it seemed that besides eating up my precious, if not otherwise spoken-for, time, Mrs. Plotsky was costing me money. Doubly determined now, I went back in the hall to give Mr. Plotsky's door a horrible beating.

But unlike his mother, he was unmovable.

2

A Trip to the Library

Mr. Plotsky, you can run but you cannot hide! My new mantra.

After drinking a refreshing cup of Tazo chai, and taking appropriate safety precautions, I rang Mr. Plotsky's doorbell—and did so every fifteen minutes to let him know just that. I donned my husband's grossly overpriced Bose headphones, specially engineered to eradicate, or greatly reduce, the thunderous drone of airplane engines, or, in this case, the Plotsky's doorbell. The custom-installed doorbell was jimmied up to be unbearably loud, from the time when Mrs. Plotsky was living alone and no amount of knocking or calling could rouse her.

Would you believe me if I told you that the Management Office, concerned about the Co-op's potential liability, sent someone from the Maintenance Department to put up a warning sign next to the doorbell? Its language is almost identical to that of the sign posted by the Cyclone roller coaster on Coney Island: "This doorbell has been classified by the American Academy of Audiologists as an EXTREME doorbell. Do not push if in the third trimester of pregnancy, have a pacemaker, or suffer from blood-pressure disorders."

Just after it'd been installed, and the sign hung, I saw the otherwise hale-and-hearty FedEx man frozen to the spot for a good five minutes, unable to bring himself to ring.

"Everything okay?" I asked him.

"Not sure. I had a physical recently and my internist said my pressure was borderline. I'm supposed to go for further testing."

I could see the guy's dilemma and felt for him. "You have kids?"

"Yeah, a boy and a girl. My little one, Shakira, she's only three," he said, tears starting to pool in his big brown eyes at the thought of leaving her fatherless.

"You're a family man. Is it really worth rolling the dice?"

He shook his head sadly. Pitying him, I signed for the package myself to spare him any further anguish. But here's the point and the last one I'll make about the doorbell: Ringing the Plotsky's bell can be an unexpected crucible in an otherwise mundane life. And how you handle it can tell you a lot about yourself, who you are, what you're made of, and can lead you to question deeply the path your own life has taken and why fate, circumstances, personal choices, and chance have, oh so cruelly, brought you to the Plotsky threshold. Or, if you're not an existentialist like Joseph and me, but religious like most people down here, it can make you cry out, if only to yourself, "Why, God, why?"

Between the first two times I rang the bell, I put the clean and folded laundry away in the dresser and took a moment as I always do to admire the unobstructed view, may it always be so, of the Chrysler building, the jewel of the midtown skyline. It's one of the two gorgeous exposures we have in the bedroom, the other one being the Williamsburg Bridge, and the East River with the sunrise at dawn, which I see daily when I get up to make Joseph's coffee and toast, and at night the moon, or like Joseph says, *la luna*. I could pinch myself I'm so lucky to live in this apartment.

As far as the laundry is concerned, I'm pleased to report that despite this morning's hecticness, I only had to pull one or two of Mrs. Plotsky's scraggly hairs off the ribbing at the top of Joseph's athletic socks. And the coverlet, as I'd thought it would be, was a perfect match.

Between the second and third time I rang the doorbell, I Googled "Jewish rites for the dead," and was relieved to find I hadn't committed any serious sacrilege. Specifically, I learned that following death "the eyes of the deceased are closed," which must've happened naturally in the dryer, because hers were sealed shut, and "the body is placed in the prescribed position." They didn't say what position, but I was pretty confident no one would have a serious argument with flat on her back. Next it said: "The dead are covered with a sheet," and it was a snap to go to the linen closet to grab a top sheet from the guest set. I took her out of the utilitarian canvas bag and spread the far-more-flattering sheet over her up to her chin, tucking it in a little on the sides. I thought she'd like that. The instructions continued: "and a lighted candle is placed near the head." Candles I have, and I got a newish one from the kitchen, the kind in the glass because Joseph's a stickler about unprotected flames, and lit it with a wooden match, improvising a prayer adapted from what I remember from Chanukah candle lighting as a child.

Barukh atah Adonai, Eloheinu, melekh ha'olam
Blessed are you, Lord, our God, sovereign of
the universe

asher kidishanu b'mitz'votav v'tzivanu
Who has sanctified us with His commandments
and commanded us

l'had'lik neir shel Mrs. Plotsky. (Amein)
to light the lights of Mrs. Plotsky. (Amen)

Back at the computer I read the final instruction. "The body is prepared for the funeral by volunteers who wash it according to ritual, and then wrap it in shrouds. The deceased is not to be left alone until the funeral." I was nothing if not a volunteer, and while I may not have washed it precisely in accordance with ritual, at least I had washed it, so she was way ahead of the game as far as that goes. As for the shrouds, my strong preference was to leave that to the experts, and with respect to the last part, where was I going?

After that, to kill time while trying to bring things to a head with Mr. Plotsky, I got to work on the flashcards. The problem with this work has been my lack of an ergonomic work area. The glass top of the kitchen table would be an okay surface, but the chair's not great to sit in for periods longer than your average meal, which in my house is twenty minutes tops, and my back, which, like my husband's, is also iffy, might seize up in a spasm. The task chair with the built-in lower back support is by the computer where it belongs, but there's no room over there to spread papers out. So I'd been putting off starting on Dolch word-list flashcard set number three when inspiration struck. I could sit comfortably on my sofa, custom ordered from Sheila's Decorating of Orchard Street, and use the luggage cart to work on. I mean for God's sake, I was already paying for it in library fines, so why not get some added benefit?

So I moved the cocktail table out of the way and wheeled the luggage cart over. Careful not to disturb the lit candle, I shifted Mrs. Plotsky's legs to the far edge where, true, they dangled off a little, and if she were alive I'd be the first to say it would not be the most comfortable position for her, but she wasn't, so I wasn't going to sweat it. Amazingly, I had most of the room I needed to stack all the peel-off Avery knock-off labels purchased from Montgomery Stationery on Grand Street between Ludlow and Orchard—not far from Sheila's Decorating come to think of it—side by side with the 3 x 5 index cards, whose price, because I had bought them in a lot of 2,000 cards, they'd knocked down from $.79 to $.59 per 100, which I don't have to tell you is a steal. When I finished making a flashcard, I just laid it on Mrs. Plotsky's stomach, and thanks to the setup of this new work station, the flashcards were practically making themselves and the words were piling up fast.

The words on the Dolch list that begin with an a are: "a," "about," "after," "again," "all," "always," "am," "an," "and," "any," "are," "around," "as," "ask," "at," "ate" and "away," and I amused myself as I made the flashcards, which was otherwise tedious, by using as many of them as I could in a single sentence about Mrs. Plotsky in a kind of spur-of-the-moment, homespun homage:

If at any time you ask around about Mrs. Lana Plotsky, all you always hear again and again, is that whenever she went away, after a short while, no one ate as well, and no one had an inkling about anything.

Okay, so it doesn't make much sense, but even so, I scored 15 out of a possible 17—not bad for an ad lib— and was about to try again when the phone rang. It was Joseph calling from a break in the action.

"Hi, honey, how are you?" I squealed into the phone, so happy to hear from him.

"Kind of bummed out actually," was his forlorn reply.

"Oh sweetheart, why? What's the matter?"

"I don't know how, but on the subway I guess, I must've rubbed up against something, though I don't remember doing it, and somehow I fucked up the back of my brand-new jacket. I'm so depressed—I can never keep anything nice even for a single day. I feel like killing myself."

Once, when I was still working and we had disposable income for extras like the theater, we went to a wonderful off-Broadway play by the playwright Susan

Yankowitz, entitled *A Knife in the Heart*. Susan's moving and thought-provoking drama is about a woman who stands by her son even though he's an assassin, and I now thought, no, Susan, that's not a knife in the heart. It's close, but getting a call like this from your husband, over a jacket that you yourself have ruined but can't tell him you ruined because he's already watching you like a hawk for any trouble signs, *this* is a knife in the heart.

"Would it cheer you up to know that I'm making a set of flashcards?"

"I thought you said you didn't have a comfortable place to work?"

"That's true, but I rigged something up. Listen, by the way, Mrs. Plotsky died."

"You're kidding. I'm reeling—Mrs. Plotsky's finally dead? Is the urine smell gone from the hallway?"

"Not yet. That could linger for a while. Like cats, you know?"

"Wow. How'd you find out? Was there a shiva notice posted near the elevator?"

"Not exactly. I'll tell you when you get home. Everything else okay?"

"Darren's back." Darren was one of Joseph's colleagues who went out on a mental-health disability. He was removed from the school for hallucinating that he was a farm animal, I forget which one, but a mammal with thirty teats being sucked dry. "He seems stabilized now."

"That's a relief." I could hear the loudspeaker in the background and some kids shouting noisily outside his classroom, his frenetic, stimulating world so foreign from my own pacific one. "Do you need to get going?"

"I should but...talk to me another minute. Are you making a reservation somewhere for dinner before the opera?"

"I thought we'd eat here; it's so much more relaxing. How about dessert after?"

"Sounds good."

"Take Darren someplace nice for lunch today, okay? Don't they have the Wednesday salmon special at that place you like? It'll give you both a lift."

"That's a great idea. Let me try and catch him. Love you."

And he was happy again and all was right with the world.

As I hung up, I caught the sound of the little ding from my computer speakers again. And another. And again, until the little ding became a sustained ring tone. When I arrived in front of my computer screen, I was horrified to see my e-mail in-box filling up with notices from the NYPL, one after the other hurtling in from cyberspace, all informing me of overdue books I knew for a fact I'd never checked out: *Auto Theft Made Easy: An Illustrated Handbook; Beating the DA's DNA Evidence;* and the clincher, *How to Build a Lucrative Real Estate Career While Working as a Security Guard.*

Ernesto, you are so busted!!!

But before I went off half-cocked, making wild allegations and threatening the building staff in the very building in which I lived, a situation which eerily paralleled what happened at my former job, which I now concede may be *part* of the reason I was no longer working there, I knew from bitter experience that I'd better have all my ducks in a row first. So while the e-mails continued flooding in at a distressingly tidal pace, I pulled my shoes back on and, knowing how untrustworthy phone transactions can be, made ready to go see the librarian personally, remembering to put my driver's license in my pocket for I.D., since as has been well-established, I didn't have my library card. I blew Mrs. Plotsky's candle out because Joseph would kill me if he knew I'd left an unattended flame in the living room. And worse, I'd probably receive a strike under the somewhat fluid rules of his Domestic Behavior Management Schema, which had been instituted since the flame-out, and was liberally adapted from "Say Yes to Good Behavior," the Department-of-Education-sanctioned disciplinary system used in his classroom.

I made for the door but stopped in my tracks, remembering, "the deceased is not to be left alone until the funeral." So I took the extra moment to remove the Dolch cards from her tummy, pulled a long parka out of the closet, and covered her with it, not because we had anything to hide but because, though a long shot, God forbid a pigeon should poop on her, I would've contributed to the desecration of the dead, and that I couldn't live with. "We're outta here!" I cried, and the door slammed loudly behind us.

Cooperative Village is blessed to be within walking distance of two excellent branch libraries, thank you New York Assembly Speaker Sheldon Silver: Seward Park on East Broadway and Hamilton Fish on Houston Street, pretty much the same distance from my building and I go to both, more or less, interchangeably. But today, because I had company, I was going to have to head to Hamilton Fish because of the stairs at Seward Park, not to mention the sharp turns and narrow passageways once you get inside.

Ernesto saw me leaving the building with Mrs. Plotsky and bellowed from down the hallway, not unpleasantly, "Where you going with the luggage cart, mami?"

"Urgent errand," I replied, hurrying out, not wishing to tip my hand. I kept my facial features neutral in case he was trailing me on the security camera. Besides, while no one is more for democracy, small d, than me, since when do I have to answer to the security guard about my comings and my goings? Since never, that's when.

"Where's she going with the new luggage cart?" I heard one of my neighbors asking the wind.

More Cooperators on the other side of Grand Street, abruptly interrupting their conversation to do so, watched me cross the street. I waved, the cart swerved, and I learned—thankfully not the hard way, no harm done—that it really takes two steady hands at all time to steer. No one waved back.

"She's crossing the street?"

"Maybe her car's parked on this side?"

"Why wouldn't she pull her car up to the door? Who crosses the street with the luggage cart?"

"I don't know. This I never saw."

"This I can't believe I lived to see. Again she's crossing the street. It's not even our property no more."

"Now she's turning? Is she leaving Cooperative Village?"

All eyes upon us, I straightened my posture and held my head high. With Mrs. Plotsky at my side somehow I was seeing the neighborhood anew, maybe through her eyes? The first thing I noticed was the bold red, white, and black graphics of the *No Dogs Allowed* sign with its encircled outline of a hyper-alert German Shepherd ready to pounce, stopped only by a damning diagonal line. So I ask you, did the Board of Directors vote to pick the drawing of a German Shepherd of all things to terrify these poor Holocaust-fraught *Juden* into submission? If so, why stop with the visual? Why not attach a loudspeaker with a pack of them savagely barking and an angry authoritarian German shouting over them, *Achtung, hund verboten, Achtung, hund verboten, Achtung...*

The flowers were eccentrically beautiful—the riot of colors, the way they jolted you back to the here-and-now, with the violet next to the orange on top of the magenta, the whole dizzying, cockamamie color scheme really adding to the already-hallucinogenic effect of living here. Picking up speed, the wind at our backs, in my heart I saluted the flapping stars and stripes as we breezed past the flagpole with its more sober amber marigolds crowded at the base, our landscaper's nod to the approaching autumn. Across Lewis Street, past the doctors' and dentists' offices, chiropractors' and chiropodists' too, we paused at the entrance to the internal Co-op park of the Hillman Houses to read with reverence the words of Stanley Hillman, the great utopian, etched in limestone: "We want a better America..." He's probably rolling in his grave now that Hillman's been privatized, and the once affordable, spacious state-of-the-art apartments he intended for teachers, nurses, and garment workers are being sold to NYU-graduated filmmakers and performance artists for half a million and up.

We raced right on by the new and dangerously steep ramp leading down, down, down to the Management Office, and made the right on Columbia Street a.k.a Abraham E. Kazan Street. Almost all our streets are doubly designated to honor mostly Jewish luminaries of yore, to make people stop, reflect, and ask, just who was this Kazan that he got a whole New York City street named after him? Obviously not chopped liver.

We moved alongside the Amalgamated Houses, the oldest and most venerable of the four sister co-ops that make up Cooperative Village, glad to have left the clamoring members of the peanut gallery far behind, with their squinting rheumy eyes and scratchy scolding voices holding forth with their every paranoid suspicion, and I had some room to breathe and think about what might be coming next.

Our local librarians make it a point to boost public awareness of published authors from the neighborhood, and one day I hope to join those ranks atop the bookshelves at Hamilton Fish, for I too have literary aspirations: I'm working on a biography-slash-memoir of my father who died in 1997, leaving behind a treasure trove of letters. He wrote the letters as a young man, away from home for the first time, in the armed forces no less, and they're addressed to his parents, brother, and their dog, Laddy. What a writer my father was. Such neat handwriting, perfect spelling and, oh my, such a vocabulary he flashed in daily missives from October 4, 1943 until October 21, 1944, sometimes more than one in a single day, all on the original U.S. Armed Forces stationery. Most impressive of all was the variety of ways

he signed off with love. While his hands down favorite
was "All my love," he also wrote:

Love to all,
Love and kisses,
All my love to all,
Love to all of you,
Love as always,
Love and accessories,
Love and stuff,
Amor a todos,
I love you all,
Loads of love,
I love you all very much,
Love to you all,
All my love always,
That's all for now my loves—
All my love as always,
My love to all,
All my love to all of you,
All my love to you all,
My love to you all,
All my love to everyone,
Goodnight, with all my love,
Love and more love,
Lovingly yours,
Love and blintzes,
Love to everyone,
Love to my loves,
Con amor,
With all my love,
Love and syllables.

There are sheaves and sheaves of letters, and I'm working my way through, making notes as I go, a project I long to get back to, and will, just as soon as I finish with Joseph's Dolch cards.

Slowing my pace to steady the luggage cart over a hazard of chicken bones on the sidewalk—the littering in this neighborhood is out of control—one of the guys leaning against the wall of the Masaryk Convenience Store, a kindred underutilized human resource if ever I saw one, said something to me that I couldn't quite catch.

"Sorry?" I asked.

"Where you taking the old white stiff?" he re-enunciated for my benefit.

In the cocoon of Cooperative Village, we rarely talk about race or define things in terms of black and white—it's more Jewish and non-Jewish—so it took me a moment to understand that it was Mrs. Plotsky he was referring to, Mrs. Plotsky's the old white stiff. No offense taken. A straightforward answer seemed best.

"Going to the library."

He scratched his crotch, spit on the sidewalk, and considered my words, but before he could respond, working on instinct, I said to this complete stranger, "Want to come with?"

"Naw," he answered, looking down. "Got to meet a fren'."

"You've got to have friends," I said with a smile, and found myself half-humming half-singing the Moogy Klingman, Buzzy Linhart hit the rest of the way to the library, surprising myself with a lump in my throat at, *"I had some friends but they're gone now,"* as I adjusted the parka and reached under it and pulled Mrs. Plotsky's sheet just a bit tighter around her.

The lights burned brightly enough inside the one-story, tan-and-clay brick building just west of Avenue D, to be visible through the inches-thick glass, stacked cube windows. The brown-painted double doors, with a simple cement overhang, were already open, welcoming all to come inside and partake of the fruits of knowledge, and Mrs. Plotsky and I easily negotiated the entrance. The senior librarian and head of the branch is an erudite African-American anthropologist, Delmar Clayton, PhD, who happens also to be a Cooperator I sometimes see working out in the gym. Normally I don't bother him with more than a quick hello, because he's usually sweating and grunting with the barbells and presumably thinking about the follow-up to his own recent book, a spellbinding page-turner about Darwin and race *and* racism published by Fairleigh Dickenson University Press.

Branch Chief Clayton was sitting humbly at the desk right out on the main floor, doing library business, and since I knew he was top banana, most likely to help me cut through the bureaucratic red tape, I decided to speak with him first. (Though who knows if he will even remember we had this conversation because he's a very busy scholar and civic leader and, I imagine, preoccupied with pressing intellectual projects and other fascinating commitments.)

"Hi, Mr. Clayton, how are you?" I said, not exactly in a whisper, but in a low tone that showed respect for the other library patrons.

"I was fine until I saw you enter the library with our

luggage cart. What gives?" he demanded somewhat more volubly, which was certainly his prerogative.

Since he's also an expert on the African Burial Ground in lower Manhattan, I gave him the shorthand version of the Jewish rites and why I couldn't leave Mrs. Plotsky alone in my apartment.

"That's all well and good," he responded, "but it doesn't explain why you have her on the cart in the first place. I unload my groceries on that cart."

So I further backtracked to the earlier events of the morning, and since he brought up the hygienic aspect, I thought it best not to mention that I had put her in the machines, because he probably wouldn't like that either.

"That's weird," he said. "I did some laundry this morning and I didn't see her in there."

"Did you use the double-load machines?"

"No. I only had a few gym clothes."

"Well that's why. You know where they installed the new television set? She was behind there, around the corner." He seemed satisfied with my explanation.

"I hate the new TV," he said. "Every time I go in someone's blasting *The Jerry Springer Show*."

"I know, me too, but Fritzy made a deal with the cable company and got the TVs for us for free."

"It's hard to challenge free," he agreed.

We were just starting to bond so I didn't want to turn the conversation to business too quickly. Let's keep it neighborly a moment or two more, I thought.

"Did you know Mrs. Plotsky?"

"Lana? Yes, I've had the pleasure. She peed on me last year in the elevator. Ruined a brand new pair of Nikes."

"That must've been before she successfully made the transition to Depends."

"If you can call that success," he quipped. We both chuckled. "You're a long way from home. Any reason?"

"Yes sir, and a good one."

Letting him draw his own conclusions, I explained to him the strange coincidence of giving Ernesto my library card to secure the luggage cart and then receiving all the overdue notices. He took off his glasses and rubbed his Basset eyes, shaking his head.

"This is serious. And unfortunately, we're seeing more and more of this."

"More and more of what?" I asked, growing even more alarmed than I already had been.

"L. C. I. T."

"What's that?"

"Library card identity theft," he said with funereal gravity. "It could take years for you to straighten out your record. Frances, I'm sorry to have to tell you this, but you may never be in the clear."

"What?!" I half-swooned and fell against the brass pole of the luggage cart, grabbing it just in time. He pulled up a chair for me and began to lay out the consequences, beyond the obvious financial ones, which were far more far-reaching than I had ever imagined. I could barely concentrate, thinking how disappointed Joseph was going to be in me, but I forced myself to tune in when he mentioned something about The U.S.A. Patriot Act.

"Mr. Clayton, I don't understand."

"My God, Frances. Aren't you aware that under Section 215 of the Patriot Act, Congress has authorized the FBI to demand library records without a search warrant. If I get an N.S.L.—"

"—A what?"

"A National Security Letter requesting your library record, I have to turn it over. I'm not saying Ernesto is letting terrorists use your library card to check out books on dirty-bomb making, but if he did, I'd have to turn the records over to the authorities."

"Mr. Clayton, are you telling me I could end up in Guantanamo because I borrowed the luggage cart?"

"Yes. It's conceivable that you could. I'm afraid so."

"Jesus. What do I do?"

"First off, we're going to cancel your card."

"Yes, yes," I urged him. "Why didn't we do that right away?"

"Try to stay calm. Damn, the system just froze." He hit the monitor with the whole of his hand. "I've got to re-boot."

While precious minutes ticked away, I couldn't help beating myself up for not staying more abreast of current events. My only excuse, and it's a poor one, is that Joseph takes the front section of the paper with him every morning to read on his arduous commute, and even though he brings it back in his knapsack, in the evening, after I make dinner, clean up the kitchen, and do other chores, I don't always read the A section as thoroughly as I should—sometimes I just glance at the headlines, sometimes not even that. I'd been living in a fool's paradise. I couldn't believe that I voluntarily gave Ernesto my library card, and in so doing, handed over my destiny, possibly even my liberty, my very human rights.

Mrs. Plotsky, there are worse things than being dead, I said to her telepathically.

"But, but...what about habeas corpus?" I asked the librarian who had swung into high gear mauling his computer, fingers flying over the keyboard, doing everything in his power to help me with damage control.

"What about it?" was his chilling reply.

So now in addition to library fines, which they can collect from me when I'm dead over my dead body, I had something else to worry about.

"Okay, you're canceled. This should staunch the immediate bloodletting."

With a bedside manner like that, good thing he became a librarian and not a physician.

"Now what?" I asked.

"You want my advice?"

"Please."

"Contact Shelly Silver's office. Mention that you live on Grand Street, East of Essex, let them know what happened, and they'll put you on the DND list."

"What's that?" I asked, ashamed of my ignorance yet again.

"Do Not Detain."

"He can do that?" I asked, surprised, realizing how foolish the question was as soon as the words left my lips.

He nodded. I stood up to go home.

"I've taken up enough of your time, Mr. Clayton. Thank you for everything."

"You're welcome, Frances. Listen, I'm not pressuring, but my wife and I were planning on driving over to Costco tonight, back around eight-ish. Do you think you'll have the luggage cart back by then?"

"The way this crazy day is going I'm not sure. But there's two of them, so you don't have to worry. You wouldn't happen to know if there's a time limit, would you?"

"Hold on, I'll check." And to my amazement, he pulled up all of management's memos which he'd scanned onto a zip drive and professionally indexed, and I mean professionally. "Nope. Nothing about a time limit in the memo."

"Okay, well it goes without saying, I'll do my best to get it back sooner rather than later."

"Understood."

"Bye, Mr. Clayton."

As I wheeled Mrs. Plotsky out of the halls of learning into the bright September sunshine, I thought: the bad news is a Federal SWAT team could descend on me at any moment to whisk me away from my darling Joseph and deposit me in a torture chamber in a desolate Cuban prison; but the good news is I don't have to rush to return the luggage cart.

Knowledge is power.

3

Jackie O and Mrs. P

ine, Mr. So-Called-President-of-the-United-States Bush, if that's how you want to play it. But be forewarned, I'll be ready for you.

Mrs. Plotsky and I were rolling back down Columbia Street when I saw the guy I had spoken to earlier standing next to another man, waving me over. Mrs. P and I crossed the street, barely avoiding being swallowed by a monster pothole. Someone should really call 311.

"I see your friend showed up. That's nice," I said as we approached.

"Yeah, we be hanging. Believe me now, son?" he asked his pal who was holding a long-necked bottle barely concealed in a brown paper bag.

"Grandma on the go-cart. For real." He screwed off the bottle cap. "This yo' moms?" he asked me before taking a swig.

"My neighbor."

"Why you taking her out for a spin?" he asked, wiping his mouth with the back of his jersey sleeve.

"Last wishes," I said, lying to avoid the energy drain of a lengthy explanation.

"Same shit as Jackie O," he said.

"How so?"

"They wheeled her 'round the reservoir up in Central Park, po' li'l shriveled-up ho in a wheelchair. But she was 'live when they did it."

"Sounds more like her second-to-last wishes," I said, and they laughed at my little joke.

"Tha's cool," said my original friend. "How's the library?" He put his foot up on the luggage cart to rest it, which would be fine with me if it weren't in the near vicinity of Mrs. Plotsky's face, and I shook my head. He took it right down.

"Not so great." They seemed interested, and I needed to process, so I told them about the situation with Ernesto and the whole enemy-combatant complication and they had quite a bit to say about that.

"Gitmo," the friend said. "I been there. Ain't no big thing."

"Are you sure? They have reports about torture, hunger strikes, inmate suicides. It sounds bad."

"Them bitches tried to break me." He spat and it arced wide, landing on an empty Cheetos bag in the gutter. "I look broken to you?"

I looked this young man of no more than twenty-five up and down and he seemed fine, better than fine, defiant and strong, though judging from the likely contents of the bottle, probably alcoholic and maybe a little depressed around the edges.

"No, you look good."

"Damn straight."

"Did they waterboard you?" I asked him. If so, he had a perfectly good reason for drinking in the street in the middle of the day.

"What's that?" our mutual friend asked.

"From what I understand, they strap you on a board and tip you back into water and keep your head submerged until you think you're drowning."

"Yeah, that's right," said the guy claiming to have been there. "Wasn't all that. I jus' held my bref."

"You caint even swim!" said my original buddy. "We was kids at the Pitt Street pool, he fell in, and was crying like a little pussy."

"Who said shit 'bout swimming, nigger?"

"Maybe I should practice holding my breath in the tub?" I quickly interjected before sparks started flying.

"You should," he agreed. "Everybody in 'merica should, cause they can take anyone they want now and 'pologize later. I do it with a stopwatch, expand my lung capacity every baf I take, case they pick me up again fo' 'nother infraction."

Another infraction. I could just imagine what that might be.

"I din't know you was in Cuba?"

"Uh-huh."

So, how come his chum didn't know? His whole story sounded fishy if you asked me.

"You smoke them contraband cigars?"

"Smoke 'em? We was rollin' 'em. You know what I'm saying? Shi-it." Maybe he did, but I didn't. "I was down

65

there when you was up in Attica," he explained when the laughing died down.

"Attica? You heard 'bout that?"

"Yeah man, your moms told my moms, and she tole me."

Soon they were comparing prison accommodations with the same attention to detail with which the vice presidents at my old job compared B&Bs in Tuscany, and while it was fascinating, with all the talk of lock-downs and solitaire, shivs and bitches—and from them too I'm sure I could learn a lot about survival, both in and out of prison—I left them to it. We said our good-byes and they were kind enough to give us a little push up an incline and get us started homeward.

Torture. "With a government like this who needs Nazis?" I said to Mrs. Plotsky when it was just the two of us again.

The closest I've ever come to being tortured, and tech-nically, it may very well fall within the definition, was my last year at the upstart home-care agency, where I was required to attend over 100 Board of Directors meetings of one kind or another in a single year. I used to fantasize about grabbing the Chairman's gavel and knocking myself out with it, not because I particularly wanted to concuss myself, but simply to get out of the pain.

We made good time getting back to Grand Street and I thought about stopping at the Pizza Shack for a focac-cia, maybe two, because I was starving for lunch—and I'm an emotional eater—but there were a couple of pit bulls tied to a traffic sign right outside and while I know they're supposed to be sweet unless trained otherwise, I couldn't chance it with my human cargo.

We passed the recently opened People Choice Pharmacy. Their punctuationally-deficient awning-bugged me so much from the get-go that I came this close to calling the folks over at our local Business Improvement District office to ask them to get their asses over to Grand Street and improve this, but I knew they had their hands full planning the upcoming 6th Annual Pickle Day Festival, so I stifled the impulse.

We crossed with the light at Rheba Leibowitz Square.

Soon we were walking past our local FineFare grocery store, where I've seen the stock boys with my own eyes move eggs around, taking them out of one carton and putting them in another. One wonders why. Needless to say, eggs I don't buy there. You know what I do buy there? Closed things, sealed things, like Seagram's Tonic water for Joseph's evening cocktail, because he needs it after a day in the Coliseum, where it's 31 lion cubs against one teacher, even though the Chancellor knows very well that class size is inversely proportional to the quality of learning. In other words—it's the whole shebang.

I had no sooner put my key in the lock of the lobby door, than Ernesto gestured me over to his console. Well, I was hungry, ergo cranky, and my shoulders were tired and achy from pushing Mrs. Plotsky over hill and dale, and there was just no way I was walking the half a city block that is the length of our lobby to talk to him.

"What do you want?" I called from where I was.

"Your library card. It's no good, mami. *Ees* not working no more."

"Oh no? Tell me, Ernesto, how on God's good green earth would you know that?" Well, that shut him right up. "Uh-huh. Later," I said, sounding a little more street-wise than I would have thought possible, and somehow, even though my angle wasn't great and I couldn't really line it up as well as I should have, I got the luggage cart stowed in the elevator for the express trip upstairs.

Of course, the first thing I did was knock on Mr. Plotsky's door to try to reason with him again.

"Mr. Plotsky, I'm sorry I was a little obnoxious before."

"A little?" he screamed through the still-closed door, his lung power completely unaffected by his surgical ordeal.

"Okay, maybe I deserved that. All I want now is to bring your mother in, so you can have the private family time you need and make whatever arrangements you think best."

"You're running all over the neighborhood with my mother on the luggage cart, in this wind, and now you think you can waltz in here and dump her back on me? In your book anything goes, no matter how nutsy-cuck-oo? I've got news for you, chicky: You found her, you bury her."

"Mr. Plotsky, you know I can't do that," I called through the peephole, trying to control my temper, won-dering how in the hell he knew about our field trip. "I can't pull a burial plot for her out of my magician's hat, and frankly, even if I could, it's not mine to do."

He was quiet for a moment and I thought, now, fi-nally, he's becoming reasonable. I heard his slippers shuffling down the hall, followed by the high-pitched screeching sound made by the scraping of the metal legs of his walker as his preponderous weight gouged deep grooves in the floor. Why am I the only one bothered by this? Aren't the neighbors downstairs driven to drink, or at least to distraction? With all the bulk on him, the gliders I had just bought him from Baron Hospital Supply on Delancey Street must have already been ground down to nubs; so on top of everything else, there was another $12 plus tax out of my pocket.

But instead of the noisy unlocking of many metal bolts and shifting gears, I only heard a slight whisking sound as he pushed a piece of paper blackened with his messy child's scrawl underneath the door. I bent down to pick up the note and was disgusted, horrified and disgusted, by the two words written there:

BURN HER!

"Fine," I said, quickly shoving the note in my pocket where his mother couldn't see it, not that she could see, but still, if this was a mother's reward, I was doubly glad I didn't have children. "I accept responsibility."

That does it, I thought, right after lunch I'm calling my lawyer. She'll know how to deal with this madman. My stomach growled as I unlocked my door and pushed the luggage cart inside. But even before I opened the fridge to see what I had in there—I couldn't even remember the last time I really shopped—first I re-lighted the candle for Mrs. Plotsky in order to restore a little dignity to the proceedings and get back on track like human beings, like good Cooperators, like *mensches* for God's sake.

So now I had my hot head cooling in the fridge with choices to make. What was I eating *for*? To bulk up for an indeterminate prison term, in which case I'd go with carbs and comfort food, or a swift, intense, but ultimately victorious battle, in which case I'd be looking for anti-oxidants. I split the difference with an egg-white mushroom omelet, a cold cannelini-bean salad, and a hunk of black-cabbage bread ($4 a loaf, from *Panetteria Falai* on Clinton and Rivington Streets, also in walking distance).

While I was cooking, I found myself looking forward to speaking to my attorney, Hope P. Hardon. A lot of hooey circulates about how Jews are the best lawyers because the Old Testament's already so legalistic, and according to stereotype, Jews are more cunning and shrewd. For my shekels, the lawyer you want, and thank God I already have, is a moral and decent Christian.

I know, I understand, they're few and far between, and not easy to find, but I'm telling you, it's worth the trouble to look, because Hope fights for me, for all her clients, like we're Jesus Christ on the cross, and fervently believes if she gives her best and her all, she's actually got a shot at getting us down off of that rickety thing. Listen to me, hear me, and someday, you'll thank me: Smart lawyers are a dime a dozen, but when you've got a big, stinking fight on your hands, what you most need is passion, and when you want passion, you call Hope P. Hardon, Esq. of Great Kills, Staten Island, New York.

I made the call and was happy to find she wasn't in court or on one of her increasingly frequent vacations—she picked right up. I presented the issues—the L.C.I.T. and the impasse with Mr. Plotsky.

"Okay, I think I understand the situation," she said,

after asking a few salient questions. "Based on what you've laid out, I can advise you. Go forward with the cremation. You've got a written authorization, a biological imperative, and frankly we need to clear the decks in case Attorney General Alberto R. Gonzales comes a-calling. I'll send someone over to pick up the corpus, I mean body. Questions?"

"Think you can get them here before 4:30? It'd be nice if she was gone by the time Joseph gets home."

"Shouldn't be a problem. We'll expedite. As a matter of fact, let me make the arrangements and call you back."

"Good idea. I'll keep the phone clear."

Just because I didn't want a Jewish lawyer doesn't mean I didn't want great Talmudic scholars mulling over my problem from every possible angle, probing the weaknesses of my case, and offering invaluable guidance, and so I decided to post my business on the Co-op Village Message Board. Others get off on porn, but as far as we, the 300 members strong of the Co-op Village Online Community are concerned, our message board is the reason the Internet was invented in the first place.

Through the miracle of information technology, and the many hours of free labor contributed by Josh Dishkin, the board's administrator, we have a powerful communications tool at our disposal, day and night. Nothing that happens within the confines of Cooperative Village goes unnoticed or uncommented upon. You no sooner hear a siren than Milty Chicago finds out where the fire was, and posts. By the time you become aware of the buzz about a new restaurant in the neighborhood, LESserEvil knows the status of its liquor license, Jewpiter has eaten there, probably doesn't like it, and they've both posted. You need a babysitter, a good exterminator, or a babysitting exterminator? The Co-op Village Online Community is eagerly waiting for you to ask so they can shove their recommendations and opinions down your throat, and even if you don't ask, if they think you need help, you'll get it anyway, like it or not.

I wrote a condensed version of my problem, starting a new thread titled "Luggage Cart Hellride to Guantanamo" and let the magic happen.

Instantaneously, GrandPoobah replied: "We already have a thread started on personnel problems with the security guards. You should re-post there."

Cooper, who everyone knows is Josh, wrote: "GrandPoobah, she's a newbie. Give her some time to get the hang of it."

Pathetique added: "Are you sure you're not just a racist? I love Ernesto. His incredibly loud whistling of the salsa classics never fails to cheer."

EssexManiac advised: "Cooper, so what if she's new? Don't enable. Let her follow the rules like everyone else."

Milty Chicago wrote: "Irving Berlin used to check out books at the Seward Park branch. Zero Mostel too, when he wasn't painting at the Educational Alliance."

OytyToity inquired: "Did they ever meet? And Pathetique, do you love Ernesto, or are you in love with Ernesto, and does your husband know?"

GrandMasterFlash disciplined the rowdy group: "Can you people please take your meds and stay focused on the subject. This Cooperator needs our help!!!!!"

I decided to take a break while they cycled through their preliminary group dynamics and built up some steam. I'd tune back in when there was a critical mass of replies.

The phone rang and it was Hope again. I grabbed a memo pad and pencil in case I needed to take notes, which it turned out I did.

"They'll arrive at approximately 4:00, no later than 4:15, so Joseph needn't get unduly stressed. Be sure to get a receipt for Mrs. Plotsky and file it away safely. To avoid confusion, begin a new file."

"Okay, I'll label it 'Neighbors Found Already Dead.'"

"And keep track of your miscellaneous expenses. I'm hoping to get you reimbursed from the estate. Can you hold on a second?"

"Sure." She put her hand over the phone, but I heard her side of the conversation anyway, because she was yelling. "The rib roast. Spoon the marinade over it, *before* you put it in the oven. Make a tent with the foil."

While she shouted out orders, I made a few notes:

Reimbursable?

Cost of laundering Mrs. Plotsky—$2.50 (no receipt)

Aggregate cost of library fines—??? (owed and unpaid)

"Sorry about that. My paralegal needed some direction. Where were we?"

"Will the cremation people take VISA?" If so, I'd get the Chase Travel Award Miles to use towards our next vacation, which would certainly help the medicine go down.

"The charge will appear as a disbursement on my bill."

"Oh, all right," I grumbled, as a slideshow of European capitols receded into the mist. "Makes sense, I guess."

"Have you signed up with Speaker Silver's office?"

"Not yet," I said, starting to doodle a circular form that, tellingly, soon shaped up to be a crown of thorns. "I'm not supposed to leave the body alone."

"Don't be a martyr," she cautioned. "Fewer than 3% of the people on his Do Not Detain list have been picked up anyway, so while it's not foolproof, it vastly improves your chances."

"I'll go after they take Mrs. Plotsky. Do you think there's a chance it could all blow over?"

"Let's hope and pray. Will the librarian let us know, as a courtesy, if the Feds request your record?"

"I don't know."

"Please ask him. Also, e-mail me your library bar code and your PIN. I'll have my paralegal start review-ing the alleged list. Frances, I know you're strong. You couldn't have survived working five-plus years for that cretin if you weren't." The managing director's *Soylent Green* memo had really stuck in Hope's Christian craw.

When Hope had represented me in matters related to my flame-out, we'd reviewed my employment history in detail. The trouble started with a three-year stint work-ing for a pioneering female arbitrageur who, when not otherwise being a tireless harridan, indulged a mother fantasy. One day, I found my in-box occupied by a Hefty garbage bag of her worn-out clothes from the 1960's, unfashionable even in their day. She also named me as a beneficiary in her will and left it lying around on top of the filing cabinet so I'd see the bequest, which was a formula: $1,000 a year for every year in her employ, but only if I was still working for her when she died. Naturally, I fled, but from there ping-ponged between the frying pan and the fire in a steady descent to the ultimate inferno of the upstart home-care agency.

"What's your point, Hope?"

"At best, you've had a checkered career. The Federal prosecutor could paint a not-unpersuasive portrait of you as a high-risk personality."

Have I mentioned that Hope can be a bit of a demagogue?

"So?"

"So, it would therefore look infinitely better for all concerned if you were to sit shiva for Mrs. Plotsky."

"*I* should have a shiva for her? Is that even Kosher?" I doodled a hangman's noose.

"It places you well within the bounds of propriety: she was 93, you discovered her already dead, you took all appropriate and necessary actions, including, but not limited to, alerting management and informing her next of kin. Said kin deputized you to cremate her. You honored the deceased in her own sacred traditions. I can make this case in my sleep."

I doodled a nuclear power-plant silo containing a stick figure named Mrs. Plotsky and, to the side, a black box with a hot-button detonator, many hands reaching for it.

"Hope, we have City Opera tickets this weekend. Joseph's really been looking forward to it."

"Don't do all seven nights. Do two consecutive. My office will arrange for the publication of the death notice. E-mail me her Hebrew name, alliterated, please. The only ancient language I read with anything approaching fluency is Latin."

"Her Hebrew name? You've got to be kidding."

"No, I'm not. I'm deadly serious. One last thing. You liked your court-ordered therapist, didn't you?"

"Serena? Sure, she was okay."

"Good. Make an appointment. Now."

"Why?"

"To give you support during the mourning process."

"I have to go back to therapy because Mrs. Plotsky died?"

"You've been breathing her in for years now, and I assure you, even if you don't understand it at this moment, you'll find her death a loss. Time will show you what kind and how much, but she has touched you and changed you and you will not be unaffected by her absence. Bless her soul."

Hope is about ten paces ahead of me in life, and I never question her counsel. I'm just glad she's still in shouting distance and I can hear her through the din, even if I have to pay $200 an hour for the privilege. So if she said dispatching with Mrs. Plotsky was not going to be an emotional slam dunk, then I guessed I'd better prepare for a few sharp elbows to the ribcage and line up an appointment with Serena, who's luckily in-network in my health-insurance plan.

However, with so many details to stay on top of, I realized I'd be well served by a to-do list, my first in months. I jotted all the items down in no particular order, before I forgot them. I could prioritize later.

1. Research Mrs. P's Hebrew name.
2. Schedule appt. w/Serena.

3. Complete at least *one* set of Dolch cards.
4. *Don't give up* on writing the memoir.
5. Ask Dr. Clayton to let us know if FBI ???
6. Return luggage cart to lobby.
7. E-mail Hope library card bar code and PIN.
8. Confer w/Hope about reporting Ernesto's scam to proper authorities.
9. Prepare a shiva notice to post near elevators. Find double-sided Scotch tape. Front closet?
10. Call 311 re: pothole on Columbia Street.
11. Remember to drink 4 glasses of H2o. At least. Daily!
12. Place food/bev. order for shiva. Discuss budget w/ Joseph. Party favors?
13. Confer w/Arcadia about dust under bed.
14. Reimburse Mr. P $1.75 in change from Mrs. P's pocket. At shiva?
15. Hightail it over to Speaker Silver's office and sign up for Do Not Detain list.
16. Spot check message board periodically for advice.
17. Pick up Joseph's shirts from Special Touch Cleaners.
18. Have sex w/Joseph. Initiate?

As I gazed over the completed list, I decided the thing that made the most sense right now was to go forward with the Dolch flashcards, because if I didn't start putting out in this department, No. 18 wasn't ever gonna happen!

4

A Dunking A Day Keeps the Torturer Away

I couldn't have been more pleased with my progress on the Dolch cards, as one complete set became two and two turned into three! I'd be kidding myself if I didn't give a lot of credit to Mrs. Plotsky, who'd been great company—super helpful and remarkably unobtrusive. Her impeccable conduct, as an almost ideal co-worker, stood in bas-relief against the behavior of my former colleagues, all high-maintenance to a one.

My only criticism, and I'm not faulting her, was that the good effects of the bleach were wearing off and I was starting to smell that odor again. It wasn't too bad yet, with all the windows flung wide open and the occasional spritz of Williams-Sonoma English Wildflower Room Freshener, but the smell was putting it to the test. Expensive at $18 for four fluid ounces? Who would say no? But it's a good product, does what's advertised, and you don't need much, so a little goes a long way. That being said, by the time the cremation crew came to pick Mrs. Plotsky up, I was pretty sure I'd be ready to let her go, if not wholly emotionally as Hope had cautioned, at least, olfactorily.

I wrapped the flashcard sets individually in clear plastic bags, tying them off with the twisties that come in the box. After I did, I had that wonderful feeling of satisfaction that comes from a job well done, as well as the relief of knowing that I'd not only averted suffering another of Joseph's strikes for non-completion of task, but could also possibly use this success as leverage to earn bonus points against future strikes.

Want to know what was also making me feel great? The kids were going to learn so much using the flashcards, and have so much fun doing it, that I could almost see their little shining faces in front of me and hear their goofy seven-year-old laughter, and I wished I could somehow communicate to Mrs. Plotsky, that because of what she'd contributed to the children's advancement, and I mean advancement literally because this is the very material they get tested on, her death had not been in vain.

I put the flashcards on the console table for Joseph to see first thing as he walked in the door, and then rewarded myself with what I hoped would be a long, relaxing soak in a hot bath. I gave myself another mild pat on the back for remembering *before* I got in the tub to bring the kitchen timer, memo pad, and pencil into the bathroom so if the spirit moved me I could start my aqua-torture training. In this Joseph and I are alike: we prepare for the worst-case scenario, hoping that in so doing, we'll ward it off—a win-win strategy.

For instance, when Mayor Bloomberg's Office of Emergency Management recently issued its *What to Do in an Emergency* brochure, we were of one mind that we'd be fools not to follow the basic instructions, especially since the Mayor had gone to all the trouble of issuing a pamphlet with a glossy cover in the first place. If you open it, as we immediately did, you'll see that inside it has maps in color with alphabetized zones and a complicated legend, and we agreed that the legend alone showed that a lot of thought had gone into making it. Was it informative? And how! We now know, because we took the time to develop a family emergency plan, (how many of you can say the same?) that in the event of a hurricane, we evacuate to Seward Park High School, where, please, not just big, but huge Hollywood movie stars like Walter Matthau and Tony Curtis were students. As I pass it in my daily excursions, I can't help thinking with a certain amount of proprietary pride, there's my home away from home, but only in case of a hurricane, which, it goes without saying, I hope we never have.

What to Do in an Emergency was very clear on one point: Every household should have a Go Bag. When I read that, I didn't think, okay, the government's given up on even the pretense of keeping its citizens safe, and now they're just coming out and saying it's every man for himself and if you have a brain in your head you'll give yourself and your family every advantage you can, like packing a Go Bag. Not at all. I just got busy and packed one. My husband, who hates an unnecessarily heavy bag, questioned me about the dental floss I'd put in with a few other toiletries, which if it weighed three ounces was a lot, and we tussled over it, but I overpowered his arguments about needs versus wants.

"Just because it's an emergency," I said, with both feet planted firmly on high moral ground, "doesn't mean we shouldn't continue to practice excellent oral hygiene. If we've lost our home in a hurricane, which, God forbid, even though we're fully insured, would already be traumatic, why compound our problems with cavities at our next checkup? If we're in the shelter and there's somewhere private to floss, I say we floss. I'm not going into the shelter system with a periodontal disease. Why should I come out with one?"

I could tell by his admiring expression that I'd scored a point towards maintaining his faith in my judgment. His good opinion of me is my ballast, and I'd be lost at sea without it.

And as of right now, I was glad we had the Go Bag sitting pretty in the front closet. Even though it's the last thing in life I'd ever want to do, if need be, I'd grab it, sprint the few blocks over to Chinatown, and hunker down in a neighborhood which, like it or not, everyone knows has its own laws, which don't even resemble ours, and where the U.S. Government has absolutely no legal jurisdiction whatsoever.

The bathwater was soft and plenty hot, and the first time I tilted my head back for a quick dunk, I got a lot of water rushing up my nose and it burned like hell. I came up sputtering, only to find that even though I hadn't heard him come in, my husband the conquering hero had returned home from the daily joust and was standing in the open doorway of the bathroom, manfully fighting with his belt buckle. It was holding its own, putting up what looked like a heck of a struggle, but my money was on Joseph.

"Honey! You got out early?" His usual time is 2:57:30 under the new contract.

"Same as always, but I caught a lift with one of the teachers," he said, unzipping and raising the toilet seat.

Caught a lift with one of the teachers? I didn't like that one little bit. I don't want my devilishly good-looking husband riding around in cars with idealistic, young, and possibly horny educators—it's far too intimate. Even if they start out discussing Everyday Math or Read Alouds, how long could it really be before, "Oh look, you've got a little chalk on your shirt, let me brush that off for you," becomes dry humping in the back seat? It's not a chance I'm willing to take, especially with an institution as fragile as American marriage, but I held off on the full-blown investigation—who is she? Is she a better driver than me?—because it was not the time or place to deal with it. But believe me, at the right time, in the right place, I will address it, because my wifely antennae were now up and staying that way until further notice.

"The Faculty Social Committee's sponsoring a Halloween party next month," he announced while peeing noisily in the toilet bowl three, maybe four feet away from me.

"Fun and fabulous. Can spouses come?"

"Just teachers. Sorry. I want you to help me get a costume together."

"Who do you want to go as?"

"Julius Caesar."

I laughed, but shouldn't have. He shot me a look.

"You'll cut a fine figure as the anti-republican dictator," I said, correcting myself. "We're talking toga, sandals, and a decorative wreath."

"What about a scepter? If it's historically accurate, I'd like to carry one."

"Hmmm. I'll look into it."

"Do you think I should have my back lasered?" he asked, having opened his shirt to gaze over his furry shoulder blade in the mirrored medicine cabinet. "To wear the toga?"

"That's kind of a big expense, honey. Maybe just have it waxed."

"Will it hurt?"

"Yes."

I dunked myself, staying down as long as I could and noted the time on the memo pad—a disappointing 42 seconds.

"What're you doing?" Joseph asked me, sitting on the now-closed toilet to keep me company.

"Practicing holding my breath. I'm timing myself and recording the results." He asked what, not why, so I'm answering what.

"What's your personal best?" He looked so tired after a long, hard day, but still he engaged with me before going off to rest, because he knows that in keeping a low profile, like I've been doing since the F.O., a person can get lonely. I showed him my pad and he just laughed at me. "Forty-two? Same as your bowling score."

I splashed him. "Don't worry about it. It's a baseline; I'll bring it up. Want to come in?" There wasn't really enough room for two, and I already knew it was going to be a no, but I just wanted to let him know he's always welcome in my dirty bathwater.

"I'll take a shower when you're done," he said, getting up and starting to pull off the rest of his clothes. "There's a bad smell in the living room. Think it might be coming from the Plotsky's?"

"Yes," I said stepping out of the tub, wondering how enervated do you have to be to miss seeing an entire luggage cart? And it's not just big and brassy, it's actual brass, which goes with nothing in our living room, where the metallic finishes are pewter or brushed nickel, so you'd think that alone would do the trick.

"When we spoke earlier, I can't remember if you said there was a shiva notice posted by the elevators or not. Because I didn't see one for her, though there were plenty of others. Isn't that weird?"

You didn't see it because we haven't made it yet, I thought but didn't say, because the man just walked in from work and was obviously exhausted. "Shower first, relax a little, then we'll talk more, okay?" I handed him a clean bath towel.

"Okay," he said gratefully.

I dressed quickly because the cremation service could make its pick-up any time now, which reminded me, I wanted to ask Joseph about the tip. I was considering the $10 to $20 range and got the cash ready, but for excellent service I could go higher. I also laid out a freshly laundered set of underwear, some yoga pants and a pullover so he didn't have to think about what to put on, or ask me, "What should I put on?" This way it'd be done, and not a topic of a boring exchange between us, and therefore one less in the accumulation of such exchanges. Kind of like the dental floss in the Go Bag, I now realized—not heavy in and of itself, but it could be that last little bit that sends your back, or your relationship, into a debilitating spasm.

I waited for him in the bedroom, where there was almost no smell at all.

Now that Joseph was home, I had to admit, I was getting excited about planning the shiva. Maybe if I entertained more, home life would be interesting for him and he wouldn't be accepting rides from adoring younger colleagues? Something to think about, and possibly even discuss with the other patrons at the Grand Spa when I get a manicure, hopefully tomorrow before the shiva, if I have time, because after today, I could use the boost.

And while I was thinking about it, I got up from resting on the bed—which I was lying on because I too could've used a nap which I couldn't take because I'd have to hustle over to Speaker Sheldon Silver's office in a little while—and combed the hair I've got left and put some lipstick on, though honestly I don't know why I bother.

How old am I? Let's just say that if I sing the lyrics from a famous pop song from my youth—*Sta-and! Nah, nah, nah, nah, nah, nah, nah, nah, nuh-nuh, nah*—and you can identify it, then you're probably in the ballpark.

Joseph ambled in, still a little wet at the base of his back—which I could see because he was wearing only a towel even though he has a selection of bathrobes, including a terry cloth one hanging on a hook in the bathroom at all times, that would've absorbed the moisture in a matter of seconds—and closed the bedroom door.

"Because of the smell," he explained.

"I know, honey, but I have to listen for the doorbell."

He opened it back up. "Who's coming by?"

"Mrs. Plotsky's getting cremated."

"Uh-huh. That's unusual for Jews, isn't it?" he asked, making his way over to his side of the bed.

"Yes. She's getting picked up from here."

"We're the pickup point? How'd that happen?" he asked, stretching out on the firm mattress and repositioning the pillows comfortably under his neck.

"Hope made the arrangements."

"Hope, our lawyer Hope?"

"Yes."

"Why?"

And I told him about finding Mrs. Plotsky dead earlier by the double-load washer and Mr. Plotsky's outrageous refusal to let her in her own home.

"He abdicated responsibility, I accepted it."

"Where is she?"

"In the living room."

I didn't tell him about Ernesto and the library card treachery. Not yet. He was lying back on the pillows with his eyes closed, so I couldn't be sure how he was taking it.

"I don't understand," Joseph said, shaking his head a little. "This isn't even your regular laundry day. What possessed you?"

To answer this honestly would have entailed an admission about ruining his jacket, which I couldn't really do. The time for that would've been when he called earlier, so now I was stuck with either telling a lie to my own husband, or deflecting the question.

"I'm not one of your second-graders. If I want to vary my routine, what's the problem, as long as the chores get done?"

"How long's she been here?" Tired as he was, he got up to scope out the situation for himself. I trailed after him down the long hall.

"Better part of the day."

"When I called?"

"She was here."

"Anything else you haven't mentioned?" Lucky for me, he didn't wait for an answer. "Why are her shoes on the wrong feet?"

"That's how she was when I found her. I was afraid if I tried to change them, I wouldn't get them on again, like when you go on a plane to Europe and can't tie your shoes when you land until after you pee a couple of times."

"What happened to her glasses?"

"Impact in the washer, I think."

"Why, did you use hot water?"

"No! Cold. I think she smacked her face against the glass door."

"You didn't even take her glasses off." He rolled his eyes.

"I'm not perfect. I'm the first to admit it."

"What else broke in there? Bones?"

"Maybe a few vertebrae in her neck. It fell back unnaturally far when I was pulling her out."

"Jesus."

"I feel badly, but does it really make such a difference? She was already dead."

"Are you sure?"

"Absolutely. I'm *pretty* sure. She was stiff, she was covered, there was a smell," I said, lowering my voice.

"Why are you whispering?"

"It's Mrs. Plotsky's last day on earth. She doesn't need this aggravation."

"Christ almighty. Cancel the order."

"What?"

"Cancel the cremation!"

"Stop yelling. Hope said it was okay, we have it in writing!" And I ran to get the note from Mr. Plotsky, but the visual of Mr. Plotsky's helter-skelter craziness made things worse.

"Frances, what have you involved us in?"

"She said we have a biological imperative! She said we have to clear the decks!"

"What's coming in for a landing? A UFO?" He threw some jeans and a pullover on and stuffed his feet in athletic shoes without socks, which in 14 years together I'd never seen, and found frightening.

"Where are you going?"

"The nearest saloon."

"What for?"

"Whiskey shots, beer chasers, one after another until I'm fucking ossified. My day was already insane before I came home, thank you very much. Where are my keys?"

I saw them on the console table, got them, and held them out. "The guy's coming any minute. $10 to $20 for the tip?"

"Since when is collecting a body a solo operation?" he demanded condescendingly. He grabbed the keys out of my hand, roughly. "$15 each." The door slammed behind him, freezing me to the spot.

My eyes focused on barges and tugboats sailing by on the river, ferries and private yachts too. I wished I could take Mrs. Plotsky down to the water's edge and give her a lovely sendoff on a skiff of her own. I'd float her down the East River until the harbor currents caught her and carried her under the Verrazano Narrows and beyond. "Bye-bye, Mrs. Plotsky, *bon voyage*." I'd call, waving an embroidered linen hanky until she was out of sight and then I'd drop it too, lotus-like, in the water.

The phone rang and I made a mad dash for it, veritably leaping over the luggage cart, which was right in my way, to snatch the receiver up. But it wasn't Joseph.

"Hey Frances, it's Josh."

"Well hi there," I said, sinking down into our comfiest armchair, already enjoying the xylophonic bell-tones of his friendly voice. "How are you, buddy?"

"Great. Have you seen the message board since your post? It's exploding, and your thread was the tipping point. I can't thank you enough."

"You're welcome. I'm just glad that my prospective incarceration generated some good buzz for the message board."

"Cingular and Starbucks have reached out."

"Josh, we've spoken about corporate sponsorship. It's a bad idea. People are weak—before long they'll be tailoring their posts to suck up with product placements and posturing, you'll lose the purity, and all your hard work will go straight to hell."

"You're probably right. Take a look though, I think the board's really pulling for you on this one. Anything

I can do for you personally?"

"Since you asked, on my attorney's advice, I'm throwing a shiva for my neighbor and I could use some help on the notice to post at the elevators."

"Sure, I'll e-mail you a template. Use the shiva wizard to fill in the basic information and then we can go over some fonts and other design details. Oh, one more thing, you don't have to physically go to Speaker Silver's office to sign up for the DND list. It's now linked to the Message Board, so you can sign on electronically. Just register with a password."

"You're amazing."

I took care of the DND list right away and couldn't resist adding my two cents in the "Personal Comments to the Speaker" section.

"Dear New York State Assembly Speaker Silver:

Thank you for providing this list, which I really hope works, because it would be extremely inconvenient for me to be detained at the present time. I was recently on jury duty and feel like I already gave at the office. Anyway, if we have to have a gang of murderous criminals at the head of our federal government illegally detaining and torturing people, it's nice to know that some of our elected officials, at least on the state level, are still trying to provide basic services.

Be well and even though I don't celebrate, I know you do, so *Shannah Tovah* and I hope you're inscribed in the Book of Life in the coming year.

Democratically yours,

Your constituent,

Frances Madeson"

I got an instant auto-reply thanking me for my correspondence and crossed No. 15 right off my to-do list. As my former boss, the managing director at the home-care agency used to say, "Nothing succeeds like success"—and for spouting bromides like this, and for successfully preventing home-health aides from earning $10 an hour to do a job he wouldn't last one single day in, they pay him almost a cool million in regular and deferred compensation per annum, so I guess he knows of what he speaks, and "nonprofit" is just another Orwellian euphemism for fleecing the public. Lucky for him, with all the other problems in society at the present time, no one's paying too much attention and he can probably ride the scam out to retirement. Doesn't make it right. Doesn't make him a good person—so I called Delmar Clayton at Hamilton Fish and he picked up right away.

"Hi Mr. Clayton, it's Frances calling."

"ESP—I was just thinking of you."

"Really? Why's that?"

"In the archives down at the African Burial Ground, we have a transcript of an oral history of a household slave who, in the course of bearing witness, explained how he got human detritus out of his master's carpets from time to time. I thought you might need to know for the luggage cart. I'm sure you want to clean it thoroughly before returning it to the lobby."

"Oh yes, of course! Please e-mail me the instructions. I'll follow them to the letter. In fact, that's why I was calling you. I wanted to let you know that if all goes as planned, I should have the thoroughly sanitized luggage cart back down to the lobby well before you need it."

"That's great news," he said. "I appreciate the call."

"I'm glad. Before I let you go, sir, has the FBI been in touch about my library record?"

"No. Not yet."

"Would it be inappropriate for me to ask you to give a shout if they do?"

"Call you? No. By the time they're requesting a list from me, they'll already be listening in on your phone line too."

"Oh, right." This is a freaking nightmare!

"But I'm in the gym most evenings. Come down and find me from time to time, and I'll keep you posted."

"Thanks again, Mr. Clayton," I said, scratching off one item on the to-do list only to make room for another: "Stop by gym evenings to see Mr. Clayton from time to time."

I called Serena and she too picked up right away. It's moments like these that you realize there are no obstacles, the path is widening before you, and you're doing exactly what you're suppose to be doing—you're in the flow.

"Frances, I'm really glad you called. What can I do for you?"

I gave her the two-minute catch-up version of finding Mrs. Plotsky.

"So, I'd like an appointment."

"I have a cancellation tomorrow at noon. I could see you then, if you'd like."

Serena's office is in the East 80s, and it takes me about an hour–ten, hour–fifteen door-to-door.

"The shiva starts tomorrow evening and I have to get the house ready, once I find out how."

"I understand. I wouldn't mind coming downtown if that would help."

"You wouldn't? Then let's meet at Full City Café on Grand and Clinton. They have new outside seating, assorted panini, and delicious soup. Yesterday, they had three-lentil."

"I love lentil soup. I also love clear soups, broths. I like bisques too. And stew, porridge—I'm mad about congee." Serena believes that people should be forthcoming about their likes and dislikes, and expresses her personal preferences freely—unusual for a therapist, I'm well aware. True, the time it takes can eat into our sessions, but I usually learn something of value, like maybe I should at least try congee? It's an acquired taste—but maybe I'd like it?

"Great. See you at noon."

I rummaged through the desk drawer to find my old datebook. I blew the thick layer of dust off the cover, flipped past all the blank pages to September and made an entry for tomorrow: *Serena, noon, Full City*, and stared at it, feeling my chest muscles tighten, and my breath grow shallow as a result.

What am I doing to myself? To-do lists, phone calls, datebooks, deadlines, multi-tasking—all high-risk, pre-flame-out activities. My God, I hadn't called Serena a moment too soon. I took my datebook out to the trash compacter and released it into the abyss. I shredded the to-do list as well and sprinkled the paper confetti down the long shaft like an early snowfall, big fat flakes fluttering onto the surprised ground.

While I was out in the hall I could hear Mr. Plotsky scraping the walker back and forth in a blizzard of activity, which was a cause for concern. What's he doing in there without adult supervision?

The elevator dinged and it was the Ashes to Ashes guys come to pick up Mrs. Plotsky. "This is creepy," one guy said to the other. "I feel like I've been here and done this."

"Maybe you're having déjà vu?" his colleague wisely asked.

They came around the corner and saw me at the open door.

"Hello, are you here for Mrs. Plotsky?"

"Yes. Have you called us before?" asked the one whose name, Sal, was embroidered on what looked like an astronaut's flight suit. His colleague was Freddie.

"No. It's my first cremation. Come on in."

"That view!" Sal said gazing out with appreciation at the Williamsburg Bridge perfectly framed in our picture window. "I never forget a view."

"How much does a place like this go for?" Freddie immediately wanted to know, a question I've learned to finesse, because finances, I do not discuss with strangers.

"With the renovated kitchen, the sky's the limit, but I'm never selling. I love Cooperative Village. Would you like to see the kitchen?"

"Why not?" they both said, stepping around a ripening Mrs. Plotsky.

"We had to take everything out. Everything. I told my husband the first night, it's either the refrigerator or me."

"My wife's after me to change our cabinets," Freddie said. "She wants knotty pine."

I didn't say anything, even though in my opinion, his wife was going straight down the aesthetic road to hell. There's something sad about city dwellers with faux-country kitchens, like they don't know who they are, or even where they are.

"And in the bedroom, we have the Chrysler Building."

"That's magnificent," Freddie whispered reverently. "MetLife, Citicorp, you've got the whole midtown skyline."

"That's the spire for the Empire State Building. Unfortunately, that building blocks it. But I told Joseph, that's my husband, we can't be greedy."

"This is the room I took her out of," Sal announced. "The body I picked up. She had a chair near the window, just like you. She was sitting there, with her hands folded in her lap, like she was waiting for me."

"Oh God. In here? Her hands were folded in here?" We'd bought the apartment from an estate, but I hadn't known the owner died in my bedroom, alone, and I wasn't so happy to find out about it now.

Joseph appeared from nowhere, carrying a dark brown, plain plastic sack that had "Seward Park Liquor Store" written all over it. There are simply no bars without a hike, and my poor darling was all wrung out.

"What's going on?" he asked at the sight of me with two strange men in our bedroom.

"These gents are here to pick up Mrs. Plotsky. I was just showing them the view."

"I'm making cocktails," Joseph said, heading for the kitchen. "Boilermakers. Any takers?"

"Sure, what the hell," Sal said. "It's the end of the workday."

"I'm driving," Freddie complained. "I'll take a splash of Perrier if you have it."

"Frances?"

"I'll toast Mrs. Plotsky," I said with forced cheer, not so crazy about the idea of Joseph wanting to drink such hard stuff so early in the day.

We waited in the living room while Joseph poured the shots, beers, and Perrier. Should I put on music? If so, what kind? A lamentation or a jig? It was a little awkward with Mrs. Plotsky amongst us, and after a couple of minutes Sal went to work pulling the sheet off to ready her for the transfer to the dolly.

"That's all right. You can keep that," I told him.

"Are you sure? It's not part of a set?" Sal asked.

"Actually it is."

"Keep it. If you're sitting shiva, you'll need to cover the big mirror."

"That mirror is perfect there. Reflects the whole bridge," Freddie said admiringly.

I aimed more English Wildflower air freshener in Mrs. Plotsky's vicinity. Sal especially seemed to appreciate it.

"That was Joseph's idea."

"What was my idea?" he asked, finally coming out to join us, carrying a tray. We took our drinks but I frowned when I saw no napkins, and went into the kitchen to retrieve them.

"Hanging the mirror opposite the bridge," I said as I passed him. I opened a can of Planter's mixed nuts, and it hissed as it released its pressure. I poured them into a plain glass bowl and took it and the supplies out to the group.

"We had to drill with a special bit and sink some anchors in the beams, but so far it's holding," Joseph was saying.

"What's that, concrete?" Sal asked, knocking on the wall.

"Thick as a brick," Joseph answered amiably. He may have knocked a couple back in the kitchen. "The good stuff," he said, raising his glass, "Mrs. Plotsky, what can I say? I'm glad the suffering's over."

He was referring to ours, not hers, I thought as I dropped my shot into my beer and guzzled away, forgetting my original plan to sip merely to be polite. She enjoyed turning our beautiful home, for which we paid plenty, into a nursing home, wee-wee pad by wee-wee pad.

Freddie frowned at his bubbly water. Maybe he wanted lime?

"To the deceased," Sal said with appropriate solemnity.

"Amen," I said, and blew out the candle like it was my birthday and her spirit was decorating my cake. "I'll need a receipt."

Joseph distributed the tips, a more than generous $20 each, a sure sign of inebriation, and they took her off the luggage cart and stood her up on a dolly, binding her with a couple of safety straps around the knees and shoulders.

"Maybe take the glasses off?" I suggested. It would be her farewell lap through her home of more than half a century, and I wanted her to look as nice as possible under the circumstances. I rushed to open the door for them, partly to be gracious, because who knew better than me how hard it was to maneuver with Mrs. Plotsky on board, and partly because even numbed a little by the booze, I was finding it upsetting to watch.

"Our condolences for your loss," Sal said.

"Thank you," I responded, really touched by his words.

"We'll pass them on to her son," Joseph said, wanting to make it perfectly clear that Mrs. Plotsky was not one of our parents. He was always very loyal to his own mother when she was alive, and dutiful to her memory in death.

"Our neighbor," I explained.

"Will he want to say goodbye?" Freddie asked.

"It's difficult to know what he's up for. He's taken it pretty hard."

"We defer to your experience," Joseph said.

"It helps with the closure," Sal advised. "In the future he may regret not saying goodbye to his mother. It can really eat you up, those kind of regrets."

"I guess we could give him the option and let him make his own decision," Joseph said.

"He won't open the door to me," I said, stepping aside, not willing to endure any more of his insults. "So if one of you wants to try, be my guest."

"I'll go," Freddie said.

"That's okay," Joseph said, downing the last of his drink. "He's my neighbor. I'll do it." And man of action that he is, he went to knock while I chewed on my lips.

"Whozit?" Mr. Plotsky asked through the door. We were slightly looped, but he sounded downright smashed.

"Joseph."

"Whassup, neighbor man?"

"They're taking your mother now."

"They're taking her now? So soon?"

"Yes. Right now." He winked at me.

"Tell them to wait a second. Please."

Joseph motioned to Sal and he and Freddie wheeled Mrs. Plotsky out in the hallway, standing her directly across from the door to her former dwelling. I released the lock on our front door and joined them out there to straighten her part and smooth down an errant cowlick with my fingers, wetting them first on my tongue.

Joseph and I drank each other in. We heard the shuffling and the awful screeching of the walker and the many locks being turned and the door, which also squeaks, finally opened.

"Burn these with her!" Mr. Plotsky cried. A torrent of Mrs. Plotsky's underclothes and polyester wash-n'-wear tunic sets flew into the hallway, garments raining down on us all, even landing on Mrs. Plotsky, who was helpless to deflect the barrage. "Bye Ma." Out came her stained and filthy bathrobe. "Rrrrgh," he grunted, and a drawerful of graying and ratty brassieres slapped Joseph in the face, who looked stricken. Misshapen shoes, galoshes, and purses beyond repair were flung into the hall and landed loudly on the ceramic tile. *"These boots are made for burning,"* he sang shrilly. A deluge of support hose, socks, and a museum-quality girdle was next. Then her winter coat, scarf, and woolen cap, all pilling and smelling like a wet Collie. "You were the best ma a son could ever have and have and have." Her enema bag, thankfully empty, and a wig, still in the plastic. "Now, get her out of here! Extinguish her finally, once and for all!

Dump her smoking ashes in the gutter where the bums can piss them down the sewer!" And he slammed the door, and screamed at the top of his voice: "AND MOST OF ALL, MA, THANK YOU FOR NOT OUTLIVING ME."

The next thing we heard, and there was no mistaking it in the reverberating silence, was the distinctive pop of a champagne cork.

We were speechless, and in front of Sal and Freddie I felt especially humiliated.

"We're only supposed to take the remains," Freddie said, kicking a wrinkled blouse out from under the wheels of the dolly.

"We'd have to charge you folks extra—" Sal started to offer to put us out of our misery.

"—You shouldn't trouble yourself. We'll make sure her things find a good home," I said, standing one foot away, at most, from the trash chute. And with the ding of the elevator, we said our final goodbyes, and the maudlin spectacle was mercifully over.

Joseph gallantly held the chute open for me while I stuffed everything down as fast as I could, wishing I was the one holding the chute handle, and he was the one touching Mrs. Plotsky's longtime possessions. For some reason, when it came time to dispose of the wig, I didn't, even though of all her things it was potentially the most flea-bitten.

"Toss it, Frances. No good can come of it."

"It's real hair. Expensive. Somebody could use it."

"Then put it where I'll never see it, please," Joseph said. "That's all I ask."

"I'm keeping this too," I said, clutching the girdle.

"Why?"

"It's an unusual item."

"It's a foundation garment from the 1950's."

"Exactly."

Back inside, I stuffed the wig right in the Go Bag and folded the girdle over a hanger in our chaotic front-hall closet. "I'm afraid to look," I said. "The luggage cart. Is there a stain?"

"Like Texas," Joseph answered.

"Damn her!" I cried.

My husband grabbed me in a hug and I buried my face in his chest and stayed and stayed there. The only reason I pulled away, when I did, was because I had to clean the mess so I could get the cart back downstairs for Mr. Clayton, whom I could not afford to alienate. "Forget about me cooking tonight," I said when I finally looked at what I was dealing with. "We can go to *El Castillo de Jagua II*, if you have cash, because they still don't accept credit cards."

"Maybe I'll have the fish," was his reply.

Every time he gets the fish, he complains it's too spicy, but I'm his wife, not his mother, so I said nothing.

He took his guitar out of its case and played scales to warm up both his hands and the instrument. I envied him his instantaneous retreat into normalcy, even beauty. I still had my work cut out for me.

Unfortunately, the carpet cleaning instructions from Mr. Clayton were embedded in a devastating account of the privations endured by 18th-century African chattel slaves, which normally I would enjoy reading, but with the time pressure, I had to limit myself to a quick scan for stain removal tips—a solution of baking soda, chlorine, and potash was jumping out at me—and I quickly mixed them, substituting Clorox for chlorine and polenta mix for potash, and spread the paste where needed.

While I worked away on the luggage cart, Joseph serenaded me. After a good 20 minutes of a seamless medley of his original songs-just-waiting-to-be-hits, he strummed a purposely discordant chord. "We should talk," he announced.

"Okay. Talk."

"That was a lot of drama."

"I know. Mr. Plotsky's exhausting. Don't forget I was in there today. He was getting a lap dance."

As soon as I said it, I realized I should not have planted the idea in his brain—the same brain that at that very moment was now contemplating, "If an old Fatty Arbuckle like Mr. Plotsky can get a lap dance, what about me?"

"I'm seeing Serena tomorrow, if that's any comfort to you. Hope's suggestion."

"Good step in the right direction. Frances, I'm scrambling all day with the kids, the parents, the administration. By the time I make it home I'm ready to crash. There's probably stuff I don't see, that I can't see. But I'm counting on you to tell me if you need something from me. I never want you to get anywhere near where you were emotionally at the end of NINNY."

Even if we had a television, Joseph wouldn't watch it because of NINNY's overbearing advertising, money that could have been spent paying the home-health aides a living wage instead of propping up the prestige of the managing director and members of the advisory board, even though many of them badly needed a good propping.

"Thanks, honey." I took a last swipe with a rag over the already gleaming luggage cart, and snapped a picture of it in pristine condition with today's paper in the shot featuring the date as well as my watch showing the time, just in case.

"I've got to take the luggage cart back downstairs. Anything else you want to say?" I asked, my hand already on the doorknob.

"I care about you. I love you. I want you to be happy."

"Me too. Back in a few."

I had to let the first elevator go by as it was crowded with a Cooperator with a bicycle, even though there's a bicycle storage room downstairs so the owners don't have to clog up the elevators with bikes, case in point, now, but I'm sure he had his reasons for not using it, even though the charge is nominal and the benefit far outweighs the cost. I had to let the second car go by as well since another Cooperator with twins was already on with her stretch-limousine-sized stroller, and she was pregnant again, already showing, and her nursing bra was leaking, which at the very least was poor grooming, and maybe indicative of more serious emotional problems.

Fortunately, by the time I made it down to the lobby, there'd been a changing of the guard and I didn't have to confront Ernesto, whom by the way I no longer considered the slightest bit genial, because honestly, I could've strangled his thick neck with my bare mitts for having given me an extra layer of stress. The evening guard handed me back my now-worthless library card, and I parked the cart where I'd found it.

"My work here is done," I said, solely for my own benefit.

At the elevator, which was, just as Joseph had said, crowded with shiva notices—it happens like that, it's called a bell curve—I couldn't help noticing that the latest trend was to have pictures, so it's not just a sea of faceless Katzes, Goldbergs and Rosensteins. I ran outside and swept Grand Street with my eyes, but, of course, the Ashes to Ashes van was long gone, which was probably for the best, because any pictures of Mrs. Plotsky taken at this point would have looked artificially posed and might possibly have constituted a criminal act, not worth chancing in my current precarious legal position. The sunset, however, was spectacular, and I gawked, with my jaw hanging open at the purple, vermilion, and orange streaks across the horizon of the western sky.

I heard a commotion in our courtyard and saw Frieda running as fast she could my way, which was not so fast because while she's nowhere near elderly, she has good days and bad, and on the bad days she walks with a cane. But she was faster than the madding crowd of Cooperators who were calling for her to be tarred and feathered. I opened the doors, which shaved minutes, not seconds off her time, and we slipped into the elevator together to safety. On the way upstairs I saw that, like me, Frieda was a little messy, covered in peanut-shell dust and flushed from all the fun she'd just had feeding the squirrels in our park, and fighting, all out, with the Cooperators yelling at her not to.

"What's that, your library card?" she asked. I realized I'd been annoyingly flicking it against my thumbnail.

"Squirrels. That's who should be on the library card, not lions. They're geniuses—just the fact that they can remember where they hid the acorns!" We reached her floor, and she was smiling at me, which made my day because it was nice to see a fellow Cooperator, to whom life has not dealt the best cards in the deck, enjoying herself. "King of the jungle, my *Yiddische tuchas*."

5

Hear the Call!

I didn't even bother taking a menu at *El Castillo de Jagua II*, because I always order the same thing: avocado salad, red beans, and for dessert, homemade flan. If Joseph got fried sweet plantains, maybe I'd pick one or two off his plate, and help myself to a big spoonful of his yellow rice, which is enough to feed a small platoon of *soldados*.

I looked around at the other dining customers, mostly working-class families from the projects bordering the Co-ops, sitting down to platters of inexpensive, home-style Spanish food, talking and laughing as they reached over each other for the hot sauce, *sofrito*, and other condiments. Though dim, the light emanating from the alternating green and white pendant lamps hanging low over the long granite luncheon counter was sufficiently ample to study the paper placemat, and

I refreshed my already detailed geographic knowledge of the Dominican Republic. In the warm and homey atmosphere, Joseph flirted with the twenty-something waitress, who in my opinion's a little bottom-heavy, but he's Italian so there you have it, engaging her in a culinary discussion.

"Papi, you got a question?"

"Yes," he said, taking off his reading glasses, "what kind of fish do you use in the fish stew?"

She called out across the 50-foot expanse of the dining room to the kitchen staff and asked them in rapid-fire Spanish about the fish. A lengthy and loud explanation came back, which she translated simply enough for Joseph.

"Fried," she said.

"Sounds good. I'll try it."

"Okay, papi." I pretended not to see him watching her backside in criminally tight jeans walking back to the kitchen. Besides, I needed him in a good mood.

"I'm working with Josh Dishkin on the shiva notice."

"That's nice," he said, still absorbed in his fantasy of following her into the kitchen to play a quick round of Hide Papi's Sweet Plantain.

"I'll tell him you said hi. And I'll take care of posting it at all three elevator banks in all four buildings."

"Uh-huh, 3 x 4 = 12," he mumbled dreamily.

"But I might need your help with moving the kitchen chairs into the living room, in case we get a big crowd."

"Don't get your hopes up—there's a lot of competition."

"I know. Would it be inappropriate to put 'light refreshments' on the invitation, I mean the notice? In small print at the bottom?"

"I wouldn't. Then it'll be a stampede. Work with Josh, do a standard notice and whoever comes, comes."

"Was she popular do you think?"

"Mrs. Plotsky? She had her cronies."

"Would you say beloved? Could I say 'beloved friend and neighbor' in the notice?"

"That's pushing it."

"As the primary mourners, we need to sit on a low bench to show that we're grief-stricken."

"But we're not."

"It's for show."

"I don't want you buying special shiva furniture."

"Who said anything about buying? I was going to look into renting a bench. It's a simple low bench, what could they charge for a couple of nights?"

"We're done talking about the shiva." He shifted uncomfortably in his seat, looking hot, bored, and bothered. "Did you call the broker about the long-term care insurance?"

"I left a message a few days ago. I guess I'll have to follow up."

"Please do. Let's lock in an affordable premium while we're still relatively young, or before one of us gets sick and we can't. If we dither, one of us is guaranteed to get Alzheimer's. If it's you, I'd like to keep you at home as long as possible, and I can't do that and be an elementary schoolteacher, at least not without staffing up."

"I'm not sick, I'm strong as an ox," I asserted, but futilely. Joseph is well aware of the limits of my strength. "And, in case you haven't noticed, I'm not demented."

"Which is exactly why we should get it now. Otherwise,

it's just you and me, and me and you. You're my safety net. I'm your safety net."

"I'll call again."

"Good. Request the literature so we can read it before we meet the broker."

"I know," I said, looking around for our food. "If I know anything, I know that."

Our meals soon came and we each sank into our own thoughts. Mine drifted aimlessly but soon settled, not surprisingly with everything we'd been through together today, on Mrs. Plotsky, and specifically I wondered: Was her corpus still intact? Did they rush her right into the crematorium, or let her relax for a while first before getting down to business?

"Oh my God!" I exclaimed.

"What?" Joseph asked.

"Mrs. Plotsky... cremation... my flame-out. Don't you see? What is cremation if not the ultimate flame-out?!"

"You may be onto something there," he said. "Talk it over with Serena tomorrow, okay? I'm eating for God's sakes. How much can one man take?"

"Sorry. How's your fish?"

"Too...something."

"*Picante?*" I offered.

"Maybe."

I really felt stirred by my insight, but the elation that comes from recognizing your own destructive patterns was short-lived, because a certain Hispanic person, who I used to think of as genial, had entered the restaurant.

"Oh no," I said, spilling my plastic tumbler of ice water all over the Formica-topped table.

"Now what?" Joseph asked, like a man chewing the last straw instead of a mouthful of yellow rice and pinto beans.

"There's Ernesto," I said passionately.

"Ernesto, our security guard?"

"Yes, I hate him. He gave me such a hard time about the luggage cart today. A whole big rigmarole."

Ernesto, who had changed out of his security guard's uniform into pleated dress slacks and what looked like a genuine cashmere V-neck sweater, took a seat at a table directly across the dining room from ours. Can you believe the nerve of him? He waved to us, his gold watch flashing on his wrist. Joseph gave him a gentlemanly salute, but I pretended I hadn't even seen him. Both waitresses gravitated towards him and started to fawn shamelessly, and his laughter, which had already been loud, became giddy with hilarity as if to say, look, look at me—who's the biggest papi of them all? Sure, I thought, he's probably an extravagant tipper with his ill-gotten library card gains.

"Switch seats with me," I said, after returning from having to get the extra napkins to mop up the spill myself. "I can't stand even looking at him."

"Let's just go," Joseph said, and looked around for the waitress and started to make the checkmark signal in the air, but stopped mid-check.

"Everything okay?"

"Not really." He leaned across the sopping table and I leaned in too.

"My balls are on fire," he confessed.

"Oh sweetheart, I miss you too. I don't think we should go so long in between. It's not healthy."

"No. Listen to me. My balls, my penis, my scrotum, they're all on fire!"

His prostate levels were fine at his recent annual physical. What could this be? "Pay the check and let's go home."

And while he was doing that, I reviewed my laundry-related actions of the morning. I remembered putting the extra bleach into the wash according to Joseph's elaborate whitening maximization scheme, but I could not call up the image of me washing the whites a second time. It became clear to me that I had no recollection of washing the whites a second time, because with the distractions of the day, which were many and unusual, I had in fact not washed the whites a second time. The most sensitive part of Joseph's anatomy was sitting in underwear so full of bleach I might as well have poured the Clorox directly onto his genitalia. At the Federal Detention Center in Guantanamo Bay, Cuba, I don't even think they would come up with such a thing.

"Was the fish that spicy?" I asked to throw him off the scent, but he's a very intelligent man, and will, in the fullness of time, realize the source of his anguish and subsequently, that I'm the culprit. And then what will happen, I simply do not know.

"I can't walk," he said out on the street. "The friction is fanning the flames. Hail a cab."

Easier said than done on Grand Street. They don't cruise our neighborhood. The only time you can get one is when, lucky for you, you happen upon someone being dropped off. He clung to a lamppost while I rushed around and tried to find a car to carry him the three blocks.

"There's no cabs tonight. Let me run and get the luggage cart," I said, tears streaming down my face.

"I can't hold on. What's that wildly painted van over there with the loudspeakers on top?"

"That's the Messiah Mobile. You want me to ask the Chabad Lubovitchers if they'll run us home?"

"Ye-ess," he groaned.

So now I found myself in the awkward position of approaching, for a big favor, people I usually make a point of avoiding. Recently one of them had accosted me to ask the usual, "Are you Jewish?," and because I was rushing, I said no, which upset my brother Sanford no end when I told him about it.

"Frannie! You denied your people?" were his exact words. But he resides in an enlightened suburb in the Berkeley, California area, and does not understand what it's like to live with the constant proselytizing—between the Jehovah's Witnesses and the Chabad, it's hard to take an uninterrupted walk down Grand Street.

"Hi there, fellow Jews," I now said, whistling a different tune. There were three of them in the van. One *davening*, one braiding his *tsitses*, and one securing bundles of brochures with rubber bands for a high-holiday leafleting campaign. "My husband's in trouble—it's an emergency, we need your help."

"Maybe your mistaking us with *Hatzoloh*, the ambulance service? It's common," said the Hasid, putting down his brochures.

"I know who you are. Who's the driver here?"

"I am," the praying guy said.

"I happen to be hosting a very nice shiva tomorrow night, and if you help us, I'll let you come to distribute your brochures, and lead a few prayers. Who knows? You might even make some progress on your monthly quota, though you understand, I can't guarantee results. I can only provide you with the opportunity. Then it's up to you and *Ha Shem*," I said, pointing upstairs to the white-bearded Yid in the sky. "Guys, the offer's on the table for ten seconds." And for effect, I started to count. "Ten, nine, eight..."

They went for it!

Fresh from his pleading with the Almighty, the pious driver energetically started the engine and a spirited choral rendition of *Am Yisroel Chai* (The People of Israel Live) blared from the speakers. I couldn't help it, but I started singing my heart out, and whether it was because of the Zionist indoctrination I received in my youth at Camp *Tel Yehudah* in the Catskills, or plain old Ashkenazi hard-wiring, I really cannot say. We made a U-turn and collected Joseph, who was barely hanging on. And then it was: *Od aveenu chai*, which means, "and still we live" all the way home, really punching the sound on the word *chai. Od aveenu CHAI, od aveenu CHAI, od aveenu, od aveenu, od aveenu CHAI.*

In the elevator, the Hasids, who were now helping me upstairs with Joseph, complimented me on my singing and invited me to a *kumzitz*, which is like a hootenanny, being held in a few weeks at the *Sukkah*, which is like a gazebo, near the basketball court.

"We'll have to play it by ear. Thanks for everything. We'll look forward to seeing you tomorrow evening."

"God willing," they said in unison.

I got my darling husband inside, put the brochures we'd been given on the console table and we stripped off his clothes right there in the hallway. I was expecting to see I don't know what, telltale signs of leprosy maybe, but his dick was a little pinker than usual, that's all. I couldn't even smell any bleach. Even so, I ran a cool bath, and then rushed to the kitchen to get some non-fat plain yogurt and spread it liberally on the affected area.

"What are you putting on me? It feels good."

"Of course it feels good, it's a milk product and it's been refrigerated." He looked at me with love, not the love of a husband for a wife, but the gratitude a patient has for his doctor who's brought needed and welcome relief. "Now sit in a cool bath. You'll be fine."

I heard him ease himself into the tub and sigh, and I exhaled.

I checked my e-mail, and the template for the shiva notice was there, so I opened it and got to work, or tried to, because Joseph called for me from the bathtub. I hurried back there.

"Bring me something to read," he requested.

"Sure," I said, and grabbed the first thing I saw which was the *Hear the Call* brochure the Hasids had just pressed upon us, subtitled, *Your Tishrei Guide.* "This looks interesting," I said, and Joseph, who has wide-ranging interests, and is a latent spiritualist, agreed.

"And my reading glasses, please?"

I retrieved them from his shirt pocket and brought them in.

"Anything else? Because I'd like to get back to working on the shiva notice and it's getting late."

"What's a *lulav* and an *esrog*?" he asked.

"Read the brochure, honey. I'm sure they explain it.

Maybe there's even an illustration."

I needn't have worried about finding Mrs. Plotsky's Hebrew name, because in Josh's shiva notice wizard, when you enter the English name, the Hebrew one pops up on the screen. Since I didn't have Mrs. Plotsky's parents' names, I couldn't complete those fields, but did the best I could, reasoning that it was a shiva notice, not an official death certificate, and who would be the wiser? Moreover, if the Almighty God, Master of the Universe, was so omniscient, he'd know I'd tried.

Josh had also sent a link to a Kosher caterer, so after I made the notice, I could order the refreshments on-line for delivery tomorrow afternoon. But first I submitted the notice to Josh, who immediately instant messengered me.

"What about an image?"

"Does it have to be of the person?"

"Let your creativity soar."

So going on instinct once again, I ran to the closet and got the girdle, laid it on the couch, which is upholstered in a beautiful slate gray mohair, an elegant background for it. I took a few pictures from different angles with my digital camera, uploaded them to the PC and e-mailed them to Josh.

"Interesting iconography. What colors do you want?"

"No color printer on this end. Let's go with black and white."

While he composed the flier, I ordered the refreshments. Please, they made it so convenient. Basically, they've bundled a few of the appetizer and dessert selections into a shiva take-out package, so for around $150, I could get a nice spread of kreplach, kishka, kasha varnishkes, latkes, rugelach, and honey cake, which was great because my good tablecloth has multi-colored flecks woven in, and these foods were all neutral colors in the beige to brown family, so I didn't have to worry about the food clashing with the linens.

My last chore in a long day of chores was to e-mail Hope Mrs. Plotsky's Hebrew name for the death notice she wanted to publish, the charges for which I supposed would also appear as a disbursement on my bill, and the bar code and access PIN for my library card, so her paralegal, who I think may be her husband, could begin the research. I felt oddly vulnerable at the thought of them scrutinizing my reading record. Since the flame-out, I've been an avid user of the public library and not all of my selections have been highbrow, but I trusted Hope not to mock me too terribly much.

With all my tasks completed, I powered down and watched the screensaver dissolve to blackness, as my thoughts turned again to the fragility of life. Will I be here tomorrow to power back on? I wondered. Who can say?

I swiveled in my task chair and looked out at the now-empty living room, which only today had been so bursting, if not with life, at least with activity. But for the completed Dolch cards, there was no tangible evidence of all that had transpired. I fondled a set now, flipping through and saying aloud words I'd grown particularly fond of while making the flashcards: "clean," "fly," "grow," "light," "open," "sleep," "warm," and "yes." Yes!

I came into the bedroom where my husband was still absorbed in reading *Hear the Call.*

"Frances, this brochure is the most astonishing flier I've read since the Mayor's office issued *What To Do in an Emergency.*"

"Are you serious?"

"It's an incredible piece."

"Does it have maps and legends?" I asked.

"No, but it has pictures and recipes. Listen to this one for Traditional Challah." And he read it to me.

"Sounds okay, but I'm not crazy about poppy seeds."

"Exactly! Nobody likes poppy seeds! They get stuck in your teeth. That's the whole point of religion. First, they give you problems you wouldn't otherwise have, and then they tell you how to fix them. They mystify everything and only they have the answers. For example, they've got a holiday schedule in here with candle-lighting times, and they're all over the map. It's completely insane. The first night of *Rosh Hashana* you light the candles at 6:35 p.m. and the very next night at 7:32 p.m. Does that make any sense at all to you?"

"Maybe it's a typo. Do they say anything about a Go Bag in there?"

"Yes, of a fashion, that's where the *lulav* and *esrog* come in. I can't wait to talk to these guys tomorrow night. What an opportunity."

"What do you mean?"

"Remember how mortified we were when we read the Mayor's brochure, how many questions we had about the meaning of what we'd read? Wouldn't it have been incredible if three representatives from the Office of Emergency Management just happened to be dropping by our home the following evening? Can you imagine the grilling we'd have given them?"

"Sure, but they're public servants and we pay their salaries. These guys are our guests tomorrow, and they've already done you a tremendous favor. Big difference. I want you to be polite to them."

"Of course, I'll be polite, but I'll be ready for them too. I'm going to take their specious arguments apart, point by point. Do me one last favor. In your travels tomorrow, could you stop by the library and pick up a copy of Thoreau's *On Walden Pond*? I want to bone up a little on scripture before they come over. Hey, did you do your shiva notice already?"

"Yes. Why?

"It's too late now, but you could've put something on the bottom like 'Special Presentation: Man v. God.'"

"Let's see how it goes. Maybe we can do something like that for the second night."

"Yeah." And soon I heard him standing in front of the bathroom mirrored medicine cabinet murmuring under his breath. "I went to the woods because I wished to live deliberately, to front only the essential facts of life, and see if I could not learn what it had to teach."

"Why don't I buy a copy," I called through the door, "that way you'll have it when you need it."

"Library's fine."

"Leave me your card tomorrow. I'm not sure I know where mine is."

"Okay." He opened the door and snapped off the light. Together, we moved through the darkness into the bedroom, took the heavy custom bedspread with its fitted corner kick-pleats and piping on the seams off the bed and pulled the silver-beaded chains, rolling down the blackout shades. "I was skeptical about the whole shiva idea, but now I'm really looking forward to it."

"But you'll be polite to our guests, right?"

"Of course!"

We climbed into bed.

"How was lunch with Darren?"

"Nice. He appreciated it."

"Did you have the salmon?"

"I did, but he's a strict vegetarian now. Says it helps with the milk production."

We both laughed.

"Pucker up, sweetheart. I'm fading."

He kissed me goodnight and I burrowed under the covers and became one with the mattress. I must've dozed off for a while, but I woke with a start in the middle of the night with an awful feeling that something was wrong. I got up and tried the lock on the front door, made sure the stove was turned off, climbed up on the step stool to check the batteries in the smoke detector—it was all fine. And then it hit me: I hadn't gone to Special Touch Valet to pick up Joseph's shirts. But it got worse from there, because I peeked in his closet, and he didn't have any long-sleeve shirts for the morning. Even though it was 2:00 a.m., I looked in his laundry bag, because I still had time to wash one out by hand and have it air dry by the morning, but there were no dirty shirts either. Which meant that despite all my efforts to toe all his lines, I'd be starting tomorrow morning with a strike.

It was because of the strikes that our sex life was stagnant at the moment, and come to think of it I was probably fortunate to have gotten the goodnight kiss. Under Joseph's Domestic Behavior Management

Schema, I could receive "marital treats" only when I had accrued enough good behavior points. (Same principle for the kids at his school, except they get a pizza party.) In our home version, a strike sets you back a good 10 points, and I seemed to be getting enough strikes that I was always behind the eightball. On the bright side, I was not required to write a letter to my parents asking them to "please talk to me about my behavior and help me learn to obey the rules." My father's long gone and my mother lives continents and a hemisphere away. When it's today here, it's tomorrow there. Hence the dispensation.

My only chance at getting any September nookie at all was to earn some bonus points, but though I had negotiated hard on the bonus-point items—and they seemed fair enough when the schedule was established just after my flame-out when I was at my most contrite for visiting disruption and upheaval upon our household—those challenges too now seemed beyond me.

Ten points are given for:
    1) Preparing homemade lasagna noodles.
    2) Memorizing names of all major Charlie Parker albums in recording-date order.
    3) Reducing weight by ten pounds.
    4) Becoming fluent in Italian.

Five points are given for:
    1) Making homemade mozzarella balls.
    2) Mastering reflexology.
    3) Losing five pounds.
    4) Getting an income-producing job.

Meanwhile there's about 12 things I can, and often do, get a strike for, and not staying on top of dirty shirt drop-off and clean shirt pick-up is among them.

I was heading back to bed when I heard Mr. Plotsky's walker screeching down the hall to his front door, though I couldn't imagine where he thought he was going at this hour. Just after his surgery, we'd had some Ambien sleepwalking incidents with him with near-tragic consequences—we found him with his head in the trash chute trying to wriggle his neck and shoulders in, and Joseph, fearing the poor man would receive a serious head injury from trash cascading from higher floors, wasted no time in pulling him out, or trying to, while he thrashed and resisted so intensely I feared for his stitches. Although I thought his doctors had taken him off the stuff, he might've gotten his hands on more. Maybe he had manipulated the lovely retarded woman into pilfering some capsules from her other clients?

I heard him out in the common hall, so I threw on my Frette robe and grabbed the kitchen trash to throw down to the always-voracious compactor. Mr. Plotsky was standing in front of the elevator in his bell-bottomed pajama bottoms, drumming with manic energy on the handles of his anodized aluminum walker. His upper stomach formed a handy shelf on which were nestled two enormous male breasts. Impossible not to stare at his bizarre, bosomy endowment—Mr. Plotsky had more cleavage than me.

I refrained from asking him why he was bare chested, but I did greet him, which is probably more than he deserved.

"Hello, Mr. Plotsky, how are you?"

"Never better. My new body-art technician's coming over. She's going to work on me."

"What are you having done?" I asked, determined not to be provoked no matter what nonsense came out of his mouth.

"Tonight's the nipple piercing. If there's not too much swelling, maybe we'll do the tattoo too."

"Have a good time. Let me know if you need anything, like new sliders for your walker."

"Please, now that I know it bothers you, I'll *never* get them! Just kidding," he quickly added, and laughed hysterically. He was definitely on something. "Hey, is your husband home?"

"Yes, but he's sleeping."

"Tell him I want that phone number he promised me."

"What was that? Maybe I can get it for you?"

"It was for some hooker he uses."

"What?"

"Just kidding," he said, collapsing in laughter. "Had you going there, didn't I?"

"Goodnight, Mr. Plotsky. Perhaps we'll see you tomorrow evening? We'll be hosting a shi—"

"—Shin-dig, that's great. People should do more house parties. Sorry I can't make it, I'm having a little gathering of my own tomorrow evening."

"Oh?"

"Wish I could've invited you guys, but it's singles only." The elevator dinged. He squeezed his nipples. "Take a last look at these babies, will ya? Next time you see 'em, they'll be bedazzled!"

6

Mothers and Marsupials

"Good morning, Josh. Hope it's not too early to call," I said into his machine. "I love and adore the shiva notice. You've completely outdone yourself with the placement of the girdle, and with the shading it looks like Mrs. Plotsky's just stepped out of it, and it's still warm from her body heat. I'm betting we'll get a lot of positive feedback. If any portion of your evening's free, please try and come by. I'm going to put these up by the elevators. Bye now and thanks again."

True to my word, I pulled on a sweater, grabbed a roll of double-sided Scotch tape, the dozen fliers fresh from the printer, and my keys, said a quick goodbye to Arcadia, who'd just arrived and was busy cleaning the kitchen, and went downstairs to post the fliers. The competition for wall space was fierce. After all, there was just a small area above the elevator Up button where you could affix the tape and, sadly, a number of Mrs. Plotsky's compadres had not made it through the night.

Lately people had started to go all out with colored specialty papers instead of a plain white or linen solid. The one with swirly clouds on a sky blue background was popular, as was a lavender surf crashing under a golden setting sun, both meant to evoke the infinite cosmos, but all too flashy if you asked me. I'm glad we went with black and white, and a symbolic, rather than representative, image—to give the people something meaty to think about when they contemplated Mrs. Plotsky's death.

When I say shiva notices, I should clarify, or expand to say death notices across the board. Occasionally, a Ramirez (or a Wong, or a Jackson) was found among the Bernsteins and the Goldblatts. But mostly it was Lenny, beloved father of Ira, Fay and Sheldon; Bessie, beloved mother of Rueven, Bertram and Aviva; and now, sadly, Mrs. Plotsky.

I don't often have a reason or opportunity to visit the lobbies of the three other buildings in our complex. Each has its little idiosyncrasies within a well-ordered uniformity: long walls of windows, high ceilings, roseate marble tiles, identical lighting fixtures of enormous lunar disks attached to upside-down tripods, a few big planters with real trees and bushes, three individual mailbox alcoves, one per tower, with low shelves for the weekly grocery store and drugstore circulars, and a glassed-in bulletin board for official Co-op notices about upcoming events, like the *kumsitz* in the *Sukkah*, information about getting flu shots, and a flier for a

"Pick Your Own Pumpkin" outing mid-October, sponsored by the Cooperative Village Seniors.

I was gratified to see that the numbers of disabled elderly were pretty much spread equally over the four buildings, and there'd been no official (or unofficial) ghettoization. Though perhaps that's unnecessary since our entire complex has been designated a Naturally Occurring Retirement Community, or NORC, by the New York City Department of Aging. Personally, I'm thrilled about it. Frieda told me just the other day that the NORC sponsored a luncheon on Sunday and showed *Mrs. Henderson Presents.*

By the time I got back to my building there were a couple of Cooperators, contemporaries of Mrs. Plotsky it would seem, gathered around the elevator taking the nightly head count—with a fair amount of tsk-tsking.

"That's nice with the *goidle* on Lana's shiva notice. Stanley always had an artistic flair."

I bit my tongue and let him have the credit, even though he didn't deserve it.

"Why a *goidle*?" the other one asked. "Was she a garment *woiker*?"

"What garment *woiker*, she was a *goidler* in a shop on Eldridge Street. Bras and *goidles* they sold. You could walk in with one tit going north and the other pointing east, and Lana'd fix you right up. You'd go in *fahkakteh* you'd come out svelte."

"I'm a little *zaftig*."

"Believe me, I noticed."

"Yeah, well it would have been nice to have a *goidle* that gave me a better figure."

"You should've gone to Lana. She'd have fitted you

in a long-line bra and a long-line panty *goidle*, and from *zaftig* you'd have become svelte, and if you'd paid cash she wouldn't charge you no sales tax."

In the elevator, I relished my good luck at having overheard their conversation. I was so glad I'd gone with my gut. So, Mrs. Plotsky had been a girdler—and from the sound of it a good one! As I inserted my key into the lock I heard the phone ringing and rushed to grab it, anxious to tell Joseph the incredible news. But it wasn't yet time for my husband's mid-morning check-in call. It was Hope P. Hardon, Esq.

"Hi, Counselor. How are you?"

"I have troubling news."

"Okay, I'm sitting down." And I did.

"The volume of activity on your library card alone is sufficient grounds to raise a red flag."

"I'm a suspect because it looks like I went to the library a lot?"

"I think we'd better prepare for an inquiry. We could have a serious problem on our hands."

"Because of identity card theft? For what Ernesto made it look like I borrowed?"

"Worse. The titles my paralegal highlighted were taken out by you."

"How do you know?"

"Because of the dates. Al Franken, Michael Moore, Al Gore, Andy Borowitz, Garrison Keillor..."

"Those guys make me laugh."

"Al Gore makes you laugh? Why?"

"He just does."

"And what's this interest in Ethel and Julius Rosenberg?"

"They lived nearby. If they hadn't been executed in June 1953, they probably would've been Cooperators. Our building broke ground the following November."

"I'll review their case."

"What?! Didn't I check out a Joan Didion book? I think she was a Goldwater Republican!"

"I saw that," said Hope. I heard her ruffling some pages. "This Edwidge Danticat book about torture in Haiti. Is it pro or con?"

"It's fiction!"

Her pen was clicking, a nervous habit, and it frightened me that she was nervous on my behalf.

"I'm going to e-mail you the entire list. Please give it to your therapist. When are you meeting her?"

"In an hour or so."

"Tell her I'm considering a psychological defense. Also, please tell her what you told me about finding Al Gore funny. Okay? I want that in the record. How's the shiva coming? Are you sitting this evening?"

"Yes. Joseph's building a special bench as a class project at school."

"Good. Keep the receipts for the lumber."

"Thanks, Hope."

Well that did it. I certainly wasn't going to risk Joseph's civil rights by checking out *On Walden Pond* on his library card. If I hurried I could get over to Bluestockings, a radical bookstore on Allen Street and the only bookstore in our neighborhood, before meeting Serena. And that's what I did—after a brief word in Arcadia's ear about dusting a little more thoroughly under the bed.

I don't usually like to shop at Bluestockings because

it's always so stuffy in there, and my sinuses prickle to life, and then comes the sneezing and the dripping. So instead of wasting precious minutes browsing, I asked the fresh-faced radical woman behind the counter where I could find Henry David Thoreau.

"Can you spell that for me?" she asked. I did, but she still couldn't find him in the computer listing the store's 4,500 titles. "I'm really sorry."

"That's okay," I said. "Is there a manager?"

"Sure." She pointed me to another even fresher-faced radical woman, named Penelope, a real radical moniker if ever I've heard one, who was on the floor, shelving books.

"Hi, where could I find a book by Thoreau, please?"

"We don't stock books by dead old white guys."

"Really? Even for a dead old white guy who wrote an important pamphlet titled *Civil Disobedience*?"

"No exceptions."

"I see you have a lot of books by Noam Chomsky."

"Yes, that's true."

"Dr. Chomsky's 78 years old."

"So?"

"He's already past life expectancy. With a policy like that, you could get suddenly stuck with a lot of inventory." Please, I thought, if this nitwit could be a manager of a bookstore, I could too, and I have absolutely no bookstore experience.

Dispirited by this unwelcome display of orthodoxy, I grabbed the first thing I saw on the Staff Picks table so I wouldn't have to go home empty-handed. I felt kind of bad using my Chase Platinum VISA, but they didn't seem to mind taking it.

"Would you like a bag?" Penelope asked.

"Oh, no," I said. "I couldn't possibly take a bag, because of the, you know, environment." I simply put it in my purse.

On my way to meet Serena I passed Jutta Neuman's leather goods store and drooled, looking at the gorgeous items in the window, pricey but everything of the highest possible quality, hand-stitched right here in Manhattan by skilled workers she pays plenty. Next I came to Congee Village and took a to-go menu. I'd just read a review by C. Menegakos in the *Grand Street News*, and C. said it was pretty good, which got me thinking—maybe a little congee for the shiva?

I stopped in my tracks to gaze in the window at Harry Zarin's, which used to be a fabric store, where, lucky for me, I had ordered my custom bedspread and headboard while it was still a humble neighborhood shop. It has since been transformed into a high-end decorating emporium, and a spotted leopard-print motif now galloped throughout the store, appearing on carpeting, upholstery, throw pillows, napkin rings, and corn-on-the-cob prongs.

Imagine my surprise when, peering through the glass, who should I see luxuriantly supine on a chaise longue but my very own court-ordered therapist, Serena. I rapped my knuckles on the window and she glanced over, checked her watch, and put up five fingers, and I couldn't fault her because she was right. She still had a few minutes before our session started. So I went on ahead, walking alone to wait for her at Full City.

Once there, I decided to take a seat outside, at a table with an umbrella, which somehow seemed more private. I put my back to the sidewalk deliberately so I wouldn't be distracted by the passing show. When Serena arrived just a moment or two later, I rose as if for a judge. She motioned me back down, and I plopped down on the more-comfortable-than-it-looks wooden slatted folding chair.

Serena looked out of place on Grand Street. She couldn't help it, she's chic. About 60 I guess, but great 60, still slim and blonde, not too much makeup on her pale, delicate complexion, but then again, just enough. She's always dressed in muted, rich colors, everything fitted and belted, and she's the kind of Manhattan woman who wears a paisley fringed shawl pinned with an antique brooch to perfection.

"Where am I? What is this place?" Though the air was cool, a few beads of sweat dotted her brow.

"You're in the western quadrant of Cooperative Village," I said slowly and deliberately. "And this shopping plaza is becoming our local piazza."

"If this is a piazza, why am I looking at barbed wire fencing around a parking lot? And who exactly is Mister Man?"

She was referring to a now-defunct barber shop, where the tattered and faded awning was still a blight. "The neighborhood's in transition," I muttered, furious at our Community Board for allowing such ramshackle travesties to front Grand Street.

"I've never been down here before, and I grew up in New York. It's a lot to take in. What's down that way?" She was pointing east, and I was hoping from her angle she couldn't see the permanently broken digital clock in front of the Emigrant Bank. It's not even the wrong time—it's just blank, which somehow feels worse.

"The Henry Street Settlement. It's historic and they just hired a new executive director for the Arts Center. We have high hopes."

"Arts center," she repeated. "And that way?" She was pointing west.

"Soho."

She smiled, and her shoulders, which had been tensed around her ears, visibly dropped.

"Is that the high school you once mentioned was your evacuation point in case of a hurricane?"

"Yes! Yes it is," I said, proud that the scaffolding had recently come down, the graffiti erased, and she could see it in all of its glory.

"Thanks. I have my bearings now," she said, taking off her watch and placing it on the café table. "Hope called me at home last evening."

"My lawyer Hope? Why?"

"She fears you're alienated. Is it true, Frances, since I've seen you last? Have you become alienated?"

I sighed. "Maybe a little. I have the list of library books for you."

"Good, she was keen on my reviewing that." I handed it to her and she put on her Versace reading glasses, gave it a cursory once-over, and frowned. "This explains a lot. A lot," she repeated, as she tucked it in her one-of-a-kind tote bag, fabricated from what looked like laminated client-session notes.

"Your bag is a very unusual item," I said.

"Thank you. A fetishist, but a regular. Wish I could say more, but my profession has the strictest possible rules concerning confidentiality. So, what's on your mind? By the way, are you deliberately letting your hair go gray?"

"Yes."

"Interesting."

She made a note with a slim, silver pen which flashed as she wrote, reflecting the day's almost lurid sunlight. It was silly, I know, but I imagined it was booby-trapped and suddenly exploded in her dainty little hand with a satisfying KAPOW!

"About my neighbor, Mrs. Plotsky. I think I've made an important connection between my flame-out and her cremation. I told Joseph that cremation was the ultimate flame-out, and he thought I might be onto something."

"Joseph who?"

"My husband," I reminded her. "Do you think there could be a connection?"

"We don't have a lot of time here, so let me just be blunt and put it out there. No. All the Mrs. Plotsky stuff, that's related to your mother. Trust me. I know mother issues. Do we have to go inside to order?"

"Yes. Go ahead, I'll hold down the fort."

"The fort? Interesting word choice. Are you feeling embattled?"

"It's an expression, Serena."

"Yes, but of what?" She raised an eyebrow. "Think about it. I'll be right back." And she took her wallet, stuffed with cash, probably from co-pays, and went inside. Still a little wobbly, she made her way through the hipsters and laptops, moms and strollers, the aged and their walkers, and as I watched her, I had an important epiphany. We, in Cooperative Village, are stronger than the average run-of-the-mill New Yorker. We can go in and out of their world seamlessly, but they falter in the face of ours.

I considered getting up and fleeing—I didn't think I was going to like this Mrs.-Plotsky-as-mother stuff one bit. I could easily see myself making a dash for it, sprinting past the hot-dog stand on the corner, past the Kosher bakeries and butchers, the 99-cents stores, and both bodegas. Run, Frances, run! I cheered for myself, leapfrogging over the bicycles parked in front of Frank's Bike Shop, deftly evading the clients staggering out of Rosa's House of Beauty, dizzy from the half-can of hair-spray used to shellac their heads in place until next week's wash and set. But I stayed put, fighting with my inner cooperator to remain open to Serena and this experience.

Serena returned with an orderly tray and extra napkins. But I remained seated.

"Aren't you going to eat?" she asked, letting her uncovered soup steam into the open air.

"No. I feel a little nauseated. But you go ahead."

She peered over her glasses at me. With her glasses on, her legs crossed at the ankles, and her pad and pen out, Serena was ready to take control of the session.

"Tell me about Mrs. Plotsky," she commanded, nimbly spooning the mushrooms out of her soup and placing them under a napkin on her tray.

"I don't really know that much about her." I paused, wondering, how could she not like mushrooms? "She was 93, an original Cooperator, widowed many years, had twin boys. Ollie lives on a kibbutz in Israel, and the other one's here. Nothing like her at all. She's petite; he's gargantuan."

"Morbid obesity is the medical diagnosis."

"Right. Humongous. Mr. Plotsky moved in to recuperate from a stomach stapling."

"Gastric banding. It's only performed on patients at least a hundred pounds overweight and takes months to recover." Serena seemed disappointed.

"Oh, and I just found out she was a girdler."

"Mrs. Plotsky, a girdler? How fascinating. Interesting mother-son dynamics around body image." And with her slender futuristic pen poised over pad, she said, "Tell me more."

"She worked in a shop on Eldridge Street and, from what I understand, had a loyal following and an excellent reputation."

"Girdling?"

"Yes."

"I love it. It's so Lower East Side. Okay, Frances, let's get to work. Give me everything you've got on girdles. Let your mind wander where it will."

I thought of what the ladies at the elevator said— from "*fahkakteh* to svelte," and from "*zaftig* to svelte"— and translated for Serena.

"A girdle holds you in so you don't jiggle all over the place. A girdle makes you appear sleeker than you are."

"Right. A girdle controls your power core, a girdle diminishes you, makes you less. What else?"

"A girdle constricts your breathing."

"Yes. It encircles and envelops you."

"A girdle pinches in all the wrong places," I said, reminding her how to speak plain English. "It gives you the illusion of being physically fit without actually being fit."

"It's not what is!" she cried. "This is terrific. Keep going."

"A girdle could give you a yeast infection," I whispered, because people around us were eating. "An ill-fitting girdle could impair your fertility."

"And who, Frances, would control, diminish, pain, delude, sicken you and/or attack your essential womanhood? What kind of a person would do that?"

"A member of the Bush cabinet?"

"Yes. Good. Who else?"

"Megalomaniacal bosses if it suited their purposes?"

"True." She added it to her list. "They're experts."

"Unethical therapists and bad gynecologists?"

"Also. I'll put them down separately. Two entirely different animals. Anyone else?"

"Did you put down pimps and madams?" an unshaven guy who was surfing the net at the next table asked, perhaps because he mistakenly thought she was opening up the discussion. He may've said it a little too loudly though, because we all got some disapproving, but compassionate, looks from the Jehovah's Witness ladies who were passing out copies of *The Watchtower*.

"No. I'll add them as well. Very good. Anyone else?"

"Could you repeat the question?" someone else asked, making the same mistake.

"What are they playing?" a retired man asked his wife. They both wore the same navy blue, woolen brimmed caps, each trimmed with a band of braiding that screamed The Workmen's Circle gift shop.

"$25,000 Pyramid, I think. Here, use the napkin. You've got latte foam on your lip," she said to him. "The upper."

"An abusive or negligent mother?" the lanky, bespectacled barista, who'd come out to clear an empty table, offered softly.

"Right again!" Serena exclaimed. "Thank you."

"What'd she win?" the husband asked his wife.

"Maybe a panini?" she said, just to give him an answer so he'd leave her alone, so she could sit in the sunshine for a few minutes and enjoy her multi-berry scone.

Serena put her pad down, and shook her hand out from all the unexpected writing. "Listen, potentially this could be a great advance for you, but at the moment it's still a head trip, and I want you to get this experientially. Are there any girdle shops still in business around here?"

I scanned the block from Hester to Houston in my inner eye. "The Orchard Corset Center's not far."

"We'll take a walk."

"What for?"

"I want to experiment—change our dynamics. Your resistance is blocking your progress. Maybe if you have an actual girdle on, we can be more productive."

I contemplated her response while trying to remember what underpants I was wearing today, because at The Orchard Corset Center, the dressing room's just a few feet of space carved out by a flimsy sheet on a droopy rope and chances were everyone would see them. Most of my underpants are perfectly presentable, even cute, but there are two, maybe three, pairs that have more going for them in the comfort department than in the looks department, and I had cause for concern.

"Are you sure GHI will pay you for this, Serena?"

"You know I can't comment on that." Serena's scrupulous about patrolling the borders of the therapist-client relationship boundary. But I had to find a way to nip this clinical trial in the bud, because I really did not want to go girdle shopping with Serena, who if she's a size six, it's a lot. Like most women of a certain age in Cooperative Village, I fluctuate between svelte and *zaftig*, but even within those fluctuations, I'll never see six.

"There's something I haven't mentioned."

"What's that?" she asked.

"When Mr. Plotsky was disposing of his mother's possessions, I might have saved one or two of the more unusual items. One of them was a girdle."

"Mrs. Plotsky's own girdle?"

"I think so. He threw it out with her other stuff."

"That's even better. As an exercise, put the girdle on at home."

"Before or after the shiva?" I asked, impatiently.

"Whenever it's convenient. See how it fits, and more importantly, how it feels—you're still journaling, I hope—and bring your notes to our next session."

"Another session?" I blurted. "Are you coming downtown again? Because I'd like to get through my father's letters in my own lifetime and with all these interruptions it's nearly impossible."

"Depends. I'm sure you're sensitive to the fact that my other clients have important needs as well."

"Is that a yes or a no? Because with the bus and a subway and the up and back and the session and a snack, which, I don't know about you, but I always need after a session, half the day's shot."

"We'll see."

That's an answer? When I'd stopped working, I'd assumed my hours and days would not be so overwhelmingly directed by others' needs and priorities and I'd finally, for the first time in my adult life, have some time for myself—but between Joseph and Hope and Serena and Mr. Clayton at the library, and Mrs. Goddamned Plotsky, everyone's got a piece of me!

"How is your mother, Frances?"

"My mother? Fine, I guess."

"Is she still in New Zealand?"

"Australia, yes, she recently became a citizen. She threw a big party for all her friends. The cake was in the shape of a kangaroo, no not a kangaroo—the small one."

"A panda?" the wife of the couple at the next table suggested.

"What are they playing now?" her husband wanted to know.

"It's an animal game. The blonde names a country and the prematurely gray one names the animals."

"Is it fun?" he asked.

"They enjoy it," she said.

"No! What's that other thing, a marsupial?"

"Koala?" the net surfer offered.

"That's not it." I hate when you know something and it isn't there when you need it.

"A billabong?" Serena asked.

"Wallaby!" I finally cried. "The cake was shaped like a wallaby."

"Was it mocha?" the husband asked.

"What do you care what flavor it was?" his wife rebuked. "You're not eating any cake today. You already had a Rice Krispies treat."

"When did you last see her?" Serena asked me.

"Personally? Not sure. She was in New York for a visit five or six years ago, I guess."

"She stayed with you?"

"She wasn't visiting me per se. She was here...doing her thing."

"What's her thing?"

"Not sure. I could ask one of her surrogate sons if you really need to know."

"She has more than one?"

"Two surrogate sons and one surrogate daughter at last count."

"Don't you have two brothers?"

"Yes."

"Does it anger you that she's replicated your family structure, but populated it with stand-ins?"

"Don't be ridiculous. Who has time for anger?"

Serena made a long note on her pad, and I swear, sometimes I don't know what flightiness comes over me, but when she turned the page I imagined that a big Anthrax cloud dusted her, and she looked so funny with the silken powder all over her face that I laughed out loud.

"Something funny?"

"Yes and no."

"Frances, has she been in touch lately?"

The sky went bright white for a moment, as I clenched my teeth against the racket of the Apollo rocketships of my childhood blasting off. My head in my hands, I had trouble making sense of Serena's question, and when

I answered, my own voice sounded foreign to my ears, like it had ricocheted in an echo chamber, losing tonality with each bounce, before seeking shelter under the umbrella outside at Full City.

"She needed some money transferred between her U.S. bank accounts, so she called me, I'm not sure…possibly…right around the whole flame-out drama, and…"

"Before or after?"

"Just before I think. It was no big deal. I took care of what she needed. No skin off my nose. A couple of calls. A couple of forms. A couple of trips to the bank. I got it done."

"I'm sure you did. Listen, I want to revisit the flame-out for a minute. Do you need a break? Want a glass of water?"

"I don't need anyone," I said while nodding yes.

"What?"

"Anything. I don't need anything." I averted my eyes from her tray. Knowing those discarded mushrooms were lying there under the napkin was making me queasy.

"Okay. Why did the Court order you to see me?"

"Because of the prosecution and the, you know, conviction."

"Remind me of some of the details."

"I clashed with the in-house chef at my job."

"Why does a home-health care agency need a cook?"

"Why indeed?" I answered, not really wanting to further exhaust myself detailing the many abuses of the public trust that riddle the non-profit sector, and which Serena, who's never worked a day in her life for anyone else, probably wouldn't understand.

"Never mind. I'm sorry I interrupted you. Please go on."

"It was hate at first sight," I declared, feeling somewhat rejuvenated by the flood of recalled anger.

"Why?"

"So many reasons. He oversalted the salads, he used far too much butter in everything else. And I can't prove it, but..."

"What? What can't you prove?"

"I don't think he washed his hands after using the bathroom."

"He didn't wash and then handled the food?"

"Yes."

Serena shuddered.

"I complained numerous times to his supervisors, both orally and in writing, directly and indirectly, with words and with body language. Ultimately, I felt forced to deal with him on my own."

"What did you do, Frances?"

"I disciplined him in a harshly worded e-mail."

"Do you remember what you wrote?"

"I may have called him a real sick-o, an oleophile. I peppered it with a few well-chosen curses. I accused him of spreading filth and disease, something, oh yeah, I told him 'For your unsanitary offenses, you should be strung up by your scrotal sac and publicly flogged.'"

"You wrote 'you should be strung up by your scrotal sac and publicly flogged' in an e-mail to a co-worker?"

"Huh-huh."

"Then what happened?"

"Because he wasn't the healthiest individual—I think he was into S & M, saucing with Campbell's soups, the liberal use of trans fats, and God knows what else—he thought I was coming onto him. I was accused of sexual harassment, and made an example of." I shrugged and threw up my hands. "Crazy world."

"It certainly is." She put her watch back on, signaling our time was up, tucked her pad and pen into her tote bag, and stood up. I counted out three fives and she took them without looking, her eyes already scanning the horizon for a familiar landmark. I saw she had no intention of bussing her tray and I hated her for it.

"Don't worry about the tray, Serena," I said, "I'll take it inside for you."

"Oh. Thank you. How do I get back to...uh...New York from here?"

For a moment I considered sending her the long way via the East Broadway stop, because she wouldn't know the difference, and maybe if she walked around the neighborhood she'd have a little more respect for what we're trying to accomplish downtown, and appreciation for the dream of cooperative living we're trying to keep alive for all New Yorkers and progressive people everywhere.

But in the end, I directed her to the nearby Delancey Street subway stop, and watched her bobbing blonde head disappear around the corner of Essex Street, her increasingly sure strides lengthening as she neared the entrance to the F train, leaving Cooperative Village, and glad of it.

7

In for a Penny,
In for a Pound

As much as I wanted to, I could not sit and linger in the sunshine reflecting upon my session with Serena, although from past experience I knew the pot had definitely been stirred and there was much still to glean. I cleared our table and then hurried next door to the decidedly un-Hallmark, completely independent Card & Gift store to shop for shiva decorations.

The main business of the store appeared to be selling New York State Lotto tickets to people who could least afford them. Somewhat incidentally, the store did have racks and racks of greeting cards, but in my experience, finding one with a matching envelope without finger marks could prove something of a challenge. Lucky for me, I wasn't shopping for cards—I was shopping for inspiration.

While looking around, inspecting the merchandise with nothing if not an open mind, I found it to be a phantasmagoria. There were at least ten gift items I'd never laid eyes on in my life, and within that group was a subset of a half-dozen that defied description, were completely impenetrable as to what they were, why anyone would find them useful or pleasing, and why they would have ended up here, of all places, in Cooperative Village.

As I shopped under the watchful eyes of the South Asian proprietors, who seemed unaccustomed to non-Lotto customers, I found the crepe-paper streamer section and grabbed the last two dusty rolls of black left over from last Halloween. With those, I purchased elegant tapered candles (also black), a small statuette of the Hindu God Shiva—which had obvious relevance—a giant box of Ferrero Rocher hazelnut chocolates in the gold-and-red foil wrappers, and a bronze plaque with a charming inscription about neighbors—*For what do we live, but to make sport for our neighbours, and laugh at them in our turn? Jane Austen*

I hurried home, making only three quick pit stops: first, to invite the Jehovah's Witness ladies to the shiva, taking a moment to write down all the particulars for them; then onto *El Castillo* for a papaya shake for Arcadia—soothing to the digestive track, which she needs because she's a worrier; and finally, to pick up Joseph's clean shirts. There were so many shirts that I was almost eligible to use my VISA to pay for them; the dry cleaner enforced a strict $25 minimum for charges, and I was just under. I looked around to see if there was a lint brush, pants hanger, any other small item for sale that could put me over, but it's not really set up for that. So cash it was.

With my Card & Gift shop purchases, Arcadia's papaya shake, and Joseph's shirts on skinny white wire hangers hooked over the fleshy part of my hand, I really had my arms full at the heavy outside door. It was awkward fishing for my keys, and something of a struggle to open the door and then a second inside door. But there was no way I was going to go to the central entrance to be buzzed in by Mr. Benedict Ernesto Arnold. In fact, as I came into the building, I didn't even look down the lobby hallway to see if he was at his station. For me, he's simply *persona non grata* until I get a heartfelt apology accompanied by a certified bank check in the full amount to clear my library card of all fines and restore my reputation within the wider NYPL community.

I rode the elevator up with the UPS man who, it turned out, was delivering several large packages to Mr. Plotsky. While pretending to fumble with my key in the lock, I was able to read the shipping labels upside-down and see they were from a computer store. This upset me because of his crack last night about prostitutes, which I'm pretty sure I recently read you can now order over the Web with a PayPal account. If true, wee-wee pads, screeching walkers, and family fights, even with all the cursing and yelling, were soon going to look like the good old days.

The seasoned UPS man wasn't thrown by the door-bell sign. After years of delivering to our building, and specifically to the Plotsky apartment, he knew to knock with the flat side of his fist and call out, "U – P – S," between knocks.

Somewhere between the P and the S, I heard Mr. Plotsky yelp with excitement. "Come on in," he bleated. "Door's open. I'll give you fifty bucks to take the equipment out of the boxes and set it up for me on the desk." I guess the UPS man took him up on his generous offer, because I didn't hear the door slam for quite a while.

When I got inside I felt badly because, all by herself, Arcadia had moved our entire king-size bed and headboard out of the bedroom to give the floor a good scrubbing. This is why I hate to say anything to her: she takes it too much to heart, invariably goes overboard, and I end up feeling guilty.

Besides a call from Joseph, who wanted to know how my session with Serena went, there was only one other message on the machine.

"Hi, Frances, Felix Brainert from the *New York Times* here."

This took me only mildly by surprise, as this was not the first time Mr. Brainert had been in touch. About a year ago, he contacted me to get a quote for an article he was writing about *The Andy Milonakis Show*, because I had direct experience with the young scamp's shenanigans on Grand Street. From what I read on the message board, because we don't have a television and I've never actually watched it, the MTV comedy features a young man who plays silly tricks on his elderly neighbors in Hillman Housing and the hilarity, such as it is, comes from watching them react—usually with profound confusion, bruised feelings, and ruffled feathers—to his stimuli.

When I first encountered MTV's rising star, he was carrying a crate of oranges which he dropped on the sidewalk, causing the fruit to scatter and roll at my feet, into the gutter and onto the street. I bent over to help him pick them up while he cried and stomped his feet. Show biz!

"Josh Dishkin told me you're primarily responsible for the outstanding shiva notice in the lobbies this a.m.," I heard Felix Brainert say in his message. "As it happens, I'm doing an article for the City section on a related topic, and would love to stop by this evening and conduct an interview. If I don't hear back from you asking me not to—even though a shiva notice at the elevator is equivalent to an open invitation and you'd risk me being affronted and taking it out on you at the first opportunity in the paper of record—I'll happen by during the regular shiva hours, as posted. Thank you."

The City section is Joseph's favorite, and Felix Brainert, besides being an obviously sweet guy and a big kidder, is an excellent journalist with a great interest in Cooperative Village. But before I answered Mr. Brainert one way or the other, I called Hope to let her know the latest developments.

"Definitely let him come," Hope advised. "We can use this to our advantage. The higher public profile you have, the harder it'll be to whisk you away to an offshore interrogation center. Try and get him to take a picture, and *please*, Frances, do your best to appear sympathetic and likable."

"Fine, but how?" I asked, the first to admit I wasn't always photogenic.

"Hold on a second, please." She covered the receiver with her hand like yesterday, but once again, because she was speaking so loudly to someone in another room,

I heard every word. "The sticker for the car inspection! Peel it and affix it to the front window. Scrape the invalid one off first. Use some Windex and the de-icer gizmo. In the cabinet under the sink. Got it?... Sorry, one of my associates needed my input on a brief."

Now she has associates?

"Bake some cupcakes like Amy Sedaris," Hope advised. "Every time you see her in the paper, she's wearing a frilly apron, displaying a tray of homemade baked goods. Dollars to doughnuts, she's not going down for sedition anytime soon."

"Okay. Fine, I'll bake."

But the fat folder with my father's wartime correspondence was right next to the bookshelf where my heart-healthy cookbooks were. And when I reached for Dr. Dean Ornish's classic *Eat More Weigh Less*, the folder fell off the shelf, fanning the letters into the air. With the windows open, letting in breezes galore, the letters went flying around the living room, like in one of those fake-snow-filled paperweights. After what seemed like forever, they finally settled, fluttering around my feet.

"Crap!" I cried, and Arcadia, who heard the commotion, came running from the bedroom, a can of Pledge still in her hand. She seemed to understand, without my saying anything, that the perfect historical record of my father's military service, lovingly preserved for over 60 years, was now a total jumble. Together we gathered everything up, trying to match Red Cross stationery and keep it separate from the U.S. Army Air Force stationery, but would I ever be sure I'd matched the correct second pages to the right letters? Disgusted with myself

I stuffed the letters back inside the folder and glimpsed a single brief excerpt from a letter written on Friday, October 8, 1943 noon, that cheered me, turning lemons to lemonade:

> We march everywhere singing such songs as "I've Got Six Pence," "Beer Barrel Polka," and *Hinky Dinky Parlez Vous.*" Which reminds me last night, I was in the Recreation Hall of the Service Club. Early in the evening a bunch of us gathered around a piano and sang so many songs. Some of them were, "Mary," "Dinah," "Margy," "I Want a Girl...", "Down by the Ol' Mill Stream," "When Irish Eyes are Smiling," and even "*Bei Mir Bist du Schoen.*"

It was as if I'd thrown the I Ching accidentally on purpose. I felt like my father, dead now almost a decade, had dropped a dime into heaven's payphone and given me a call. In turn, I called the Juilliard School of Music and placed a last-minute order for a student pianist willing to bring his or her own electric keyboard down to Grand Street to informally lead us in a few standard tunes. If there's a better way to unify a disparate group of guests than a singalong through the American Songbook, I don't know what it is. As an added incentive, I threw in the carfare. Damn the cost—we're going to give Mrs. Plotsky a shiva to remember!

I asked Arcadia to stay an extra hour, for extra pay of course, to help me decorate for the event. Together we festooned the mirrors and glass-covered artwork with sheets and cloths bordered with black streamers, which we scalloped—Arcadia's idea, and a good one. We placed the tapers, unlit for the present, in three separate sets of candlesticks and positioned them around the room. We tried the Shiva statue in a few positions and ended up with it on the long countertop where the food would be displayed. The bronze plaque with the inscription from *Pride and Prejudice* we put outside near a basin of water and paper towels, required by ritual, so the mourners could wash a little before entering the shiva. This way, with the plaque there, they'd have something interesting to read while they scrubbed up.

Arcadia and I looked around and were generally pleased with the cleanliness of the room, and the few and tasteful additions to the décor, but we agreed something was missing.

"Flowers?" Arcadia suggested.

"Exactly right. I'll order a nice spray. All white, I think." She nodded. Her English was very limited and I may have lost her on spray. But no matter, I was really enjoying working with Arcadia. "Where should the keyboard go?"

"What," she asked, "is a kibbord?" So I mimed a pianist. After a quick scan of the room, she pointed to the area in front of the suite of picture windows, which was, of course, absolutely right. There's an electrical outlet right there and the musician would be backlit from the bridge lights.

Next, we dug out the platters from the back of the kitchen cabinets and companionably washed and dried them while listening to a little Nina Simone. My selection of serving pieces wasn't great, so I took out my white porcelain Passover Seder plate, which hasn't been used for its original purpose in quite a few years, but which is a nice size for entertaining a crowd. We placed a layer of doilies on top so the Hebrew lettering was barely visible, and when the platter was covered with food I was confident its intended use would become a total non-issue.

Arcadia was about to change out of her embroidered slippers back into her street shoes when I asked if I could hire her to come back and do the serving and washing up this evening. Fortunately, she was available.

After she left I ordered five portions of congee, the minimum for delivery, which seemed excessive, but they assured me it would freeze if we didn't use it all. Then I called my florist.

"I want white roses, baby's breath, pussy willows, everything white, a few spider mums for punctuation and freesia for scent. And please do an urn-shaped glass vase and fill it up halfway with white pebbles."

"Nice touch. Any message?" my florist asked. "Birthday, or anniversary wishes?"

"It's a shiva for Lana Plotsky. Surprise us." The doorbell rang. "Thanks a million. Bye." I hurried to the door. "Who is it?" I called as I peeped.

"Liquor store."

"I'm not expecting a liquor delivery." I opened the door because I recognized the guy from Warehouse Wines. Winter, fall, summer, spring, he wears the same flak jacket and duck hunter's cap.

"It's for your neighbor," he explained. "See the sign?"

Mr. Plotsky had scrawled a note saying he was napping and that we'd sign for it. Actually it was just a crooked arrow pointing our way. The note was adhered to the front door with a jagged piece of surgical tape it looked like he'd torn with his teeth.

"It's been paid for, I assume?" I asked, reviewing the packing slip.

"Yes, ma'am."

But there was the matter of the tip, which I guess now I had to shell out. I had a five in my pocket and handed it over.

"This is for you. Could I get a receipt though, for reimbursement?"

"Sure."

"You can leave the box right here," I said, pointing to a spot just inside the door.

"It's chilled. It really should go right into the fridge or a cooler."

"What!? Oh, for God's sakes. You better bring it then. Follow me." And I led him to the kitchen and waited to hear him gasp, which he did. Everyone does. It's gorgeous and no one with a pulse is immune. "How many bottles?" I asked moving some things around inside the refrigerator to make room.

"A case."

"A whole case of white wine?"

"Bubbly."

"How many guests does a case serve? Never mind. Don't answer that. None of my business." Could Mr. Plotsky be any more irritating, clogging up my fridge when I'd soon have a catering delivery of my own? I knew the cranberry applesauce for the potato latkes would have to be chilled. And I couldn't leave out the sour cream, either.

The delivery guy opened the package with his box

cutter and handed me the bottles as I placed them on the shelves, head to toe, toe to head, to make more room.

"That's all of them," he said.

"Good, cause I'm running out of…something," I complained, straightening up and feeling a little ping in my lower back, never a good sign.

"It's got a lot of capacity," he said, patting the side of the fridge.

"Thanks. The shelves pull out, and it's got two smaller crisper drawers instead of one big one."

He nodded his approval. On the way out, he must've noticed the covered mirror.

"Are you sitting shiva?" he asked.

"Couple of nights. We'll see how it goes tonight."

"Lucky," he said. "Last year, my wife and I sat for her mother. You know the low bench? By the seventh night my sciatica was so inflamed, I was popping Aleve 'round-the-clock. Cost me a couple of days' pay. My doctor said no lifting."

"That's rough."

"Death's a pain, that's for sure."

At the door we shook hands, and my smaller, smoother hand was enveloped by his big knobby, rough one.

"I'm sorry for your loss," he said.

"Thank you." My eyes welled up with tears. "You're a very kind man."

"Do me a favor, give my wife a call and tell her that," he said, wheeling his dolly to the elevator. "She says I'm a doofus."

"Wives don't always know," I called after him, closing the door and locking up.

While pulling the mulling spices out of the pantry, I called Joseph's cell phone and thoroughly enjoyed hearing his voice on the outgoing announcement—he sounded like such a New Yawker. I cleared my throat and left a message.

"The session with Serena was confusing. She wants me to experience Mrs. Plotsky more bodily, and exercise with the girdle. I'll explain later. I hope you're going to take a car service home; I can't see you squeezing the bench onto a crowded subway.

"Also, please make sure they sand it down as well as their little seven-year-old hands can sand, leaving no litigiously dangerous splinters. Our liability insurance's capped at $500,000. If you need cash for the driver, I'll meet you downstairs." I blew him a big kiss into the phone. "Mmwha!"

I measured out the nutmeg and cloves, counted out six cinnamon sticks and put them, along with the cider, in a big pot on the simmer burner.

As for baking, I had a peck of fresh-picked New York State apples, and decided to keep it simple and do a couple of trays of those. The next twenty minutes were spent washing and coring the apples. Then I stuffed raisins and honey inside the hollowed-out cores, dusted them with cinnamon, and drizzled vanilla extract on top. I covered the Corningware with Saran Wrap, as I wouldn't be baking until an hour or so before the guests were scheduled to arrive.

I sorely wanted to check the online message board, but it was either that or a hot bath with only a few minutes to spare for the drills, which I could only neglect doing at my own peril. Given the stakes, I got the bathwater started and retrieved the supplies: timer, memo pad, pencil. While the tub was filling I shaped my nails with an emery board. The manicure I'd hoped to get had fallen by the wayside. Fine, if the *New York Times* takes a picture, I'll fold my hands in my lap, and if I look demure, so much the better.

Holding my breath under the bathwater was strangely meditative. In the uncluttered space, what bubbled up was genuine excitement that the *Times* was coming to Cooperative Village tonight, especially since the visit wasn't real estate related. Yes, our apartments were deeply discounted compared to the Manhattan market, and true, they had doubled in value within the past four years, but there was more going on here than the price per square foot and incredibly cheap maintenances! It was those other things I wanted Mr. Brainert to hear about while he was in my house. Since I'd already be feeding him the three Ks—kreplach, kishka, and kasha varnishkes—I wanted to give him something else chewy and yummy to digest, something to make him, and his readers, feel good all over.

The phone rang, and luckily I'd brought the portable in with me.

"It's me," Joseph said.

"Hi, honey. Where are you?"

"Downstairs," he said. "They won't let me in with the shiva bench."

"Who won't let you in with the shiva bench?"

"I can't say. She's standing right here," he whispered. "She says it's furniture and I need a move-in pass from the office."

Busted by Trisha Phizer of the Management Office,

a real stickler, who happens to live in Building Z. How unlucky could we be? "She's got us on a technicality. Tell her it's art, not furniture. Try that," I said, standing up and starting to dry off.

"I can't. I already admitted it was a shiva bench. Anyway, she's nobody's fool. Can you come down?"

"I'll be right there."

I noted my last time, 1:17, and drew an uptick on my progress graph before stepping out of the bath. I dressed in a whirlwind, throwing on some casual clothes, and rode down the elevator with my hair still wet, smoothing it with my fingertips.

Joseph was leaning against the lobby wall, the bench propped up by his side half-bracketing him. He held out a paper crowded with text.

"She gave me a warning."

Is it horrible to admit I was a little glad? He'd been handing out strikes so cavalierly lately, maybe now he'd know what it feels like.

"Let me see." It was a long citation, but I can speed-read in a crisis and was able to summarize in no time. "They'll be watching the security camera on our elevator bank, so we can't try anything."

"I can't carry this thing up the stairs, Frances."

"No," I agreed. We're on a high floor. "But they're not watching the elevators in Building X. Let's take their elevator up to the roof, cross over on top, come back in our tower and walk down a few flights of stairs. We should be able to manage that."

"That's why I married you," he said, picking up one end of the simple but elegant bench.

"It's beautiful," I told him, as we trudged to the middle elevator bank. "The boys and girls did an excellent job."

"It was great. They learned about right angles. We examined braces and discussed stress and support. We talked about wood and where it comes from, why some nails are short and some are long, the importance of wearing safety glasses. Everyone got their own piece of sandpaper and took a turn. We discussed craftsmanship and mastery, weatherproofing and termites. Mrs. Plotsky gave us a good lesson."

"So you had enough cash for a car service?"

"I got a lift."

"Another lift?"

"No. Same teacher."

We put the bench down while we waited for the elevator.

"What does her husband say about her giving rides to distinguished and dapper male colleagues?" I whispered because there was a nanny with her young charges waiting for the elevator too. She had a mass of braids pressed under an orange tie-dyed bandana; the boys had forelocks hanging down under their Spiderman yarmulkes.

"She's young, she's single, answers to no one. She's experimenting."

He threw one hand up in the air to give his words a visual flourish, smiling broadly just at the thought of her freedom. The nanny, who had excellent hearing, rolled her eyes at me. In sympathy, I think.

"She asks your opinion about dating and boyfriends, that kind of thing?" I asked Joseph.

"Sometimes. It's fun," he admitted, "though I don't think she follows my advice. Mostly I'm just an ear."

"Uh-huh."

"Oh, Jah," the nanny said, unconvinced.

We all got on the elevator and Joseph and I both pushed the top button at the same time, though Joseph then leaned on Door Close because the doors are timed to shut at the far edge of human patience.

"What floor?" Joseph asked the nanny.

"T'ree, please." It was a quick but noisy ride with the kids begging her to make them a mango-lhassi yogurt-drink when they got upstairs.

"I cannot do it. Dinner tonight's *fleishik*, not *milchik*, and we're eating early. Maybe tomorrow," she said with a dazzling smile, proffering a little hope. The kids took the disappointment pretty well. "T'ank you," she said to us, over her shoulder, shepherding her precious little lambs off the elevator.

"Take care," I said.

"My kids had a blast with the Dolch flashcards you made," Joseph told me when the doors closed again. "Only three more sets to go and every group of four will have their own."

"I'll get to it as soon as I can."

"I know you've got your hands full," he said.

At the penthouse we carried the bench up a steep flight of stairs to the roof and found the fire door propped open with a cement block.

"I'll stay here with the bench, while you make sure the other staircase is accessible," I offered. He soon came back.

"It's open. Let's go."

We were walking over the springy tar roof when I slowed down.

"You okay?" Joseph called back, feeling the drag on his speed.

"We've never been up here. Since we are, let's see what we can see."

We put the bench down and leaned over the high wall, beaming at our three-dimensional jigsaw puzzle of a city rolled out before us, twenty-something stories below. It was windy up there, but exhilarating windy, like being on the upper deck of a boat sailing to the very place you most want to be going. We were a few weeks away from Daylight Savings Time, and there was still plenty of intense golden light in the rapidly changing sky. A few smokestacks belched blackness in the far distance, but we filled our lungs with fresher air. The humble bench was inviting; we moved toward it, and eased ourselves down. It held!

"This is nice," Joseph said. "Just to sit for a minute."

"Especially with you, Joseph."

Sitting side by side, watching the billowing clouds float by at eye level, I don't know who leaned into who first, my husband, or me, but we reached for each other, our arms entwined, held fast by each other's warm lips.

"Francesca, *mi amore.*"

Shiva Me Timbers!

"Did you get a chance to pick up the book I wanted?" Joseph called from the bedroom, where he was relaxing a few minutes before the anticipated onslaught. I was in the kitchen spooning honey syrup over the baking apples, stirring the hot mulled cider, which smelled glorious, putting toothpicks in a shot-glass-cum-toothpick-holder, fanning out my cocktail napkins, and doing the million little things a hostess must do to show her guests she cares.

"It's a long story," I called to him, heading back there, "but I couldn't get my hands on exactly what you wanted. I got you this instead." I dug the book I'd bought him out of my bag and handed it to him. "Looked interesting."

He examined it and snorted.

"*Cunt?* You brought me *Cunt* instead of *On Walden Pond?*"

"Bluestockings didn't carry any Thoreau," I said, feeling the flutter of panic that usually accompanies an imminent strike.

"I thought you were going to check it out of the library. I'm not reading this," he said, tossing it back in my direction.

"Why not? It was on the Staff Picks table," I pleaded.

"Look at the cover, Frances."

"The cover? It's...a flower, bright colors. Oh my God. You think it could be—"

"—Radical chick-lit."

"Sorry. I was rushing to meet Serena. I must've let my guard down."

"That's okay," he said with atypical magnanimity. "I'll check the Web. *Walden's* in the public domain: maybe someone's posted it online. Have you seen my reading glasses?"

I found them easily on his bedside table, inches away from where he was, grabbed them, and held them behind my back.

"I'll give them to you for three bonus points," I said, shocking myself, but going on instinct, nonetheless.

"What!?" he said bolting upright, immediately regretting that he'd shown mercy.

Seeing the effect of my simple request, I realized instantly what a house of cards his Domestic Behavior Management Schema really was. I hadn't even had to read a word of *Cunt* for the forces of female empowerment to begin surging through me. We were in a whole new ballgame.

"You heard me, honey. You want the glasses, or not?"

He blew out a long stream of air, hissing through his teeth in the process, and came to a grave decision. "Two points. And not a point more."

"Done." I tossed the glasses onto the pillow closest to him and went back to my chores with renewed energy, humming what I think may have been the tune to "*Hinky Dinky Parlez Vous.*"

And then it was a blur of ringing and knocking, assorted deliveries and handing out tips, setting Arcadia to work on arranging the platters and plates, and showing the musician where to set up. The apartment was thrumming with industriousness and focused concentration.

Joseph got dressed, and he looked incredible: charcoal gray slacks, light blue shirt, a black sports coat that draped beautifully over his broad shoulders, and an Ike Behar tie that pulled it all together. He didn't clash with the furniture in the slightest, which was more than I could have even thought to ask for.

I'd left my own outfit to the last minute and struggled with the contents of my closet. I knew Hope wanted me to go for a retro-suburban housewife look, but I didn't possess a single dirndl skirt, cashmere twin-set, or belted shirtdress. What I did have was black. I settled on a slim woolen skirt with a conservative back slit, a knit top with a Peter Pan collar, pearls with a silver clasp, nude hose, and black suede pumps. But to my horror, when I slipped the skirt on, it barely zipped and my tummy pooched out more than I would have liked under normal circumstances, but at an intolerable level if this evening did in fact become memorialized in the Sunday *Times*.

I was about to go back to the drawing board when I remembered Mrs. Plotsky's girdle folded over a hanger in the front closet, and it occurred to me that I might be able to kill two birds, very much in need of killing, with one Latex stone: Serena's therapeutic assignment and my desperate fashion challenge.

When I hurried out to get it, I saw Joseph had his guitar on his knee and was rhythmically strumming "Honeysuckle Rose" perfectly in synch with the lovely, young Juilliard virtuoso, whose beautiful auburn hair was in a French twist, and whose fingers were flying over her Casio WK8000, as her classically trained, ballet-slippered foot pumped the air, searching in vain for the non-existent floor pedal. I waved as I sailed by, but they didn't even see me, much less reciprocate, and I didn't press it. Joseph's a very serious and accomplished musician, and I'm well aware that accompanying seven-year-olds on yet another chorus of "Home, Home on the Range" doesn't totally fulfill his ambition.

The girdle, thankfully, was one-size-fits-most, and though I had to lie on the bed to pull it on, pausing at regular intervals in which I caught my breath and slowed the panting, I was, in time, able to stand, and with practice, eventually walk a little, if only mincing, geisha-like steps. As I made my way to the full-length mirror, I sucked my throbbing thumbnail, which had been painfully bent back by poor positioning under the elastic waistband. But the reflected results were nothing less than fabulous: I was svelte from the front, svelte from the back, and most incredibly, svelte from the side. I could not have been readier to sit shiva!

By the time I got out to the living room, it was a

packed house already in full jam. Our living room was bursting with Cooperators. I tried to do a quick head-count, and kept losing my place in the sea of mostly white hair, but it was somewhere around 30 guests, with five narrow bodies on the sofa alone. Joseph had brought in the kitchen chairs and set up some narrow folding chairs usually stored in the chaotic front-hall closet, and folks had organically arranged themselves in intimate groupings within the larger circle. As I surveyed the proceedings, I could catch snippets of conversations, mostly of a medical nature, plus the requisite heavy bragging about grandchildren, or in one case, a combo.

"My granddaughter, the logician, who graduated first in her class from M.I.T., has a post-graduate fellowship at The Technion Institute in Haifa."

"I didn't know she was in Israel," her neighbor complained. "Since when? Last I heard she was a consultant to NASA."

"Maybe you weren't at the NORC meeting when I passed around the postcard of the Wailing Wall? What you also don't know is she recently donated one of her kidneys to save a Palestinian child's life. A stranger she didn't even know. Was it logical? Maybe, maybe not. Are we proud of her? I could bust."

Maybe the girdle was making me more emotional than usual, but I got a lump in my throat and had to fight back tears.

The Hasids, I was sorry to see, having already papered the house with the *Hear the Call* brochure, were off by themselves examining our CDs in a wall-mounted shelving unit. From their body language, I could tell they were making derisive comments about our collection, which I admit is eclectic but very solid in the Bebop era.

At the buffet line, one of the few Italian-American ladies in attendance was getting an explanation from her Jewish girlfriend, who looked like she could be her sister. Same teased and sprayed white hair, same bejeweled Coke-bottle glasses, and similar, though not identical, housecoats.

"What are those?" the Italian-American woman asked, pointing to the kreplach.

"Like a dumpling, but with Kosher meat and spices inside."

"Something like ravioli?"

My stomach rumbled when she said ravioli, and embarrassingly and unexpectedly, the sound was amplified, not muffled, by the girdle.

"More like perogi. Try it." The Italian woman unenthusiastically put one on her plate.

"What's that fuzzy brown stuff on the pasta?" she then asked, pointing to the kasha varnishkes. "I never saw *farfalle* prepared like that."

"Kasha. It's a grain. Take a spoonful, but be careful. It can be a little oniony."

She tasted it. "No garlic?" she asked, confused. "Are those cookies?" she asked, pointing to the round circles of stuffed derma.

"No," the Jewish lady laughed. "It's kishka, it's delicious. Better you shouldn't know exactly what it is. Just eat it. It won't kill you."

Carefully, I lowered myself down to the empty mourner's bench, though between the limitations in

movement caused by the girdle and the extreme low-
ness of the bench, I did not so much sit as lean, one foot
braced on the floor at all times for balance.

A woman sitting nearby struck up a conversation
with me as she picked at a piece of honey cake.

"You're the hostess?"

"Yes."

"And that's your husband over there?" she asked
pointing at Joseph, who saw us and smiled.

"That's him."

"How long you know each other?" she asked, scraping
the almonds off the top of the cake with her fingernail.

"Almost 15 years."

"How'd you meet?"

"At a bar-b-que, when I lived uptown."

"He was grilling?"

"No," I laughed. "We were both guests."

"You liked him from the first?"

"Yes. You're very intuitive. I was drawn to him, and
I guess he was to me too, because we immediately
made a date for a SummerStage concert two weeks
later."

"Your first date was a free concert in the park?"

"No, because before even one week went by, he called
to say we shouldn't wait."

"Really? That you don't hear too often. So where'd
you go?"

"A Picasso show at the Guggenheim. We started at
the top and before we spiraled all the way down, we
were holding hands."

"That's a beautiful story. You went for a bite someplace after?"

"Yes. Near the museum. I ordered guacamole."

"Good."

I started to ask her something about herself, but she'd already turned to the woman on her other side and repeated the story, adding embellishments as she saw fit. Instead of the Guggenhiem, she placed us at the top of the Empire State Building and, in her version, guacamole became a Turkey Club Deluxe with onion rings, not fries.

Everyone, some familiar faces from the mailboxes and bus stop, some strangers just waiting to become friends, had shown up ready to get right into the swing of things. The good spirit was palpable. In the break between songs, one fun but palsied Cooperator told a joke, the telling of which I would've enjoyed more if he hadn't been waving his hot mulled cider around quite so perilously.

"What did the 95 year-old alter kocker say to the sexy prostitute when she offered him super sex?"

"How should I know?" asked one of Mrs. Plotsky's girlfriends who was sporting her special occasion blue, white, and gold-sequined bandana. "What'd he say already?"

"I'll take the soup!"

We all howled at the punch line, though my laughter, constricted as it was by the girdle, sounded more like a whinny than a guffaw.

"What'd he say? I couldn't hear," she cried. Her friend repeated it over and over, but she never did get it.

Next, one of the Lubovitchers pulled out a slender ebony recorder and joined Joseph and the pianist in "It Was A Hot Time in the Old Town Tonight" and everyone sang, just slightly adapting the lyrics to suit the occasion:

Late one night, when we were all in bed,
Old mother Plotsky left the lantern in the shed,
And when the cow kicked it over, she winked her
    eye and said,
There'll be a hot time in the old town tonight.

Arcadia passed a tray of kreplach without the dipping sauce, as I'd instructed, because I'd recently had the carpet professionally cleaned and even though I'd shopped around, it cost a fortune. She also made sure everyone took a cocktail napkin, as I'd also asked her to, and she had a precautionary bottle of club soda standing by in case of spills. The all-white floral bouquet was splendid in the candlelight and the room veritably twinkled in the twilight. The oven timer dinged and I willed myself to levitate off the low bench to take the baked apples out of the oven. I happily placed them in the warming drawer, noisily dropping them the last few inches because I could not bend over that low. The warming drawer's a feature I don't get to use nearly often enough, but I did now because why rush people to eat what was basically a dessert item while Arcadia was still out passing the hot hors d'oeuvres?

I heard the recorder in a long solo of "Sunrise, Sunset" from *Fiddler*, sure to be a crowd pleaser, and should not have been as surprised as I was when Joseph came up behind me and grabbed my hips.

"You look fantastic," he whispered urgently in my ear. "I love your outfit."

"Honey, you've seen it a hundred times."

"You look different. Amazing. You're so shapely, so womanly tonight. What's your secret? You're making me crazy. I want to bend you over the kitchen table and have at you. Let's go in the bedroom."

"Stop it, silly. Somebody could become disoriented and wander in."

"I don't care. Where are you on the points thing, baby?"

"Deep in the hole," I said, to inflame him.

"Want to make a quick 10 bonus points?"

"Who wouldn't? But how?"

Even as my body was aroused by his overtures, my brain slapped my docile, limp wrist for ever buying into this counterfeit point setup in the first place. Ten bonus points flying in on a magic carpet, appearing out of nowhere, on Joseph's say-so!

But my libratory impulse was short-circuited when he whispered the raunchiest thing I've ever heard him say in 14-plus years of intimacy, right in my ear, scorching the Tympanic Membrane, and I don't even want to admit how horny I got. Serena was going to have a field day with this journal entry, if I could ever bring myself to write it down.

I'm ashamed to say I don't know how far we would have gone if we hadn't been interrupted by the terrible screeching of Mr. Plotsky's walker, which we could hear above the animated conversation, above the Broadway show tune, above even the sounds of our own wildly booming hearts. We peeked out the kitchen doorway to see the dreaded Mr. Plotsky and his filthy, corroded walker, framed in the front door, a vision from Mad Max.

"Hello everybody. My name is June. What's yours?" and he blew the crowd a kiss.

He was still shirtless, and his nipples, which were the size of teacups, were plastered with tiny mirrored beads. He'd changed out of his pajama bottoms into some drawstring pants and he was barefoot, but that's not all. He had also applied some bright red lipstick, barely staying within the contours of his fleshy lips, making his teeth look sunflower yellow, and around his neck he sported a violet feather boa. It was like Divine from *Pink Flamingos* had dropped by, but, you know, a computer-aged version.

The pianist, thinking this was part of the act, struck the chords of the rousing intro to "Let Me Entertain You," and Mr. Plotsky high-stepped, to the extent he could with the walker and his elephantine ankles, in time with the timeless anthem from *Gypsy*.

"My parquet floors!" I cried to Joseph. "He must be stopped."

"Stanley, did you wash your hands in the basin outside?" one of his mother's canasta partners yelled at him. "Because they look *schmutzadich*."

"I like your hat," Mr. Plotsky said to one of the Lubavitchers, who was wearing what looked like a small opossum on his head. Mr. Plotsky winked at him and the Hasid blushed. "Don't get your knickers in a twist, I'm here for my Bolly. Baby June wants her Bolly."

"What's he talking about?" Joseph asked me.

"His champagne's chilling here; Bollinger's I guess. Help me put the bottles back in the case," I said, moving quickly towards the fridge.

"Champagne for what?"

173

"He's having his own soirée."

"Tonight?"

I shrugged helplessly. Tonight? Every night hereafter? Who knows? His presence had really changed the atmosphere, and not for the better.

"This is nothing," one of the neighbors was now declaiming in the living room. "I remember when he was just a little pisher, he'd imitate the Rat Pack, all of 'em, all at once. He'd croon, then he'd tap, then he'd belt—he was a marvel. Now this. I'm glad his mother's not here to see. She'd be broken-hearted."

When we got back in the living room with the heavy Warehouse Wines box, Mr. Plotsky was at the buffet, helping himself to a bowl of steaming congee. "What is this, risotto?" he asked, sticking his finger in the communal pot to taste. "But runny?"

"I'm going to be sick," I whispered to Joseph. Needless to say, congee was no longer in the cards for me.

"Here's your champagne, Mr. Plotsky," Joseph said. "C'mon, I'll walk you back."

A younger man, relatively speaking, who'd been sitting attentively the whole time holding a spiral-top steno pad on his lap, now rose and asked Mr. Plotsky, "Are you related to the deceased?"

Could this be Felix Brainert of the *New York Times*, with a little kasha on his tie?

"Who wants to know?" Mr. Plotsky correctly asked. And when he answered, it turned out my guess was right—it was Mr. Brainert. The room grew quiet, and the easygoing flow and exchange of conversation and kibitzing stopped abruptly.

"You're the big shot Neighborhood Correspondent.

You live around here somewhere, but you're not a Cooperator, right?" a gruff voice from the crowd asked.

"I'm priced out. Journalists don't really earn the kind of living you need to buy a whole Manhattan co-op. At best, I could afford a closet or two."

I thought he was perfectly charming, but others obviously didn't agree.

"You know why they don't pay you very much? Because you're a lazy bum!" the man who'd told the joke sneered, while gumming a latke.

"No I'm not," Mr. Brainert said, obviously wounded. "Why do you say that?"

"Because you only write about the neighborhood you live in. Why are you here anyway?"

"I'm doing a follow-up piece on the story I broke about competitive bar-mitzvahs," he said, with a good amount of journalistic pride. "I'm investigating whether the same level of exorbitant spending and professional party-planning is happening at this stage of the life cycle."

The crowd groaned.

"He thinks maybe Lana Plotsky flew us in on her private jet from Gstaad?" There were titters.

"This guy's even a bigger *putz* than I thought," someone behind me jeered.

"I read your article about decorative manhole covers. I'm sorry to tell you this to your face, but it was superficial. Woodward and Bernstein would have at least opened one."

"They're heavy," Felix said in his own defense. "Some of them weigh almost—"

"—So you bring a crowbar, you pry it open and climb down into the sewer to see what's what. Then you'd

175

have a story. You understand me? You have to probe beneath the surface."

"Writers—feh! If they're not making things up in their screwy heads, they're copying from other people."

"Mr. Brainert, do you know my son-in-law had to hire a lawyer at $400 an hour to help us fill out the application for Medicare Part D? A simple drug benefit from my own government, and regular adults couldn't make heads or tails of it. Maybe you hadn't noticed, but we're old."

"Speak for yourself," probably the oldest woman in the room called.

"Sorry Hannah. *Some* of us are old," the speaker corrected herself. "We're on a fixed income, which is meager and inadequate for our basic needs."

"Tell him, Goldie," someone shouted.

She continued. "Some of the Cooperators you see here are healthy, knock on wood." Everyone, including Joseph, leaned down and rapped on the floor. "But others of us are very, very sick, and without our medications we would either die right away, or...or, we would suffer, more than we already suffer. Are you with me?"

"Old, poor, sick," Brainert repeated.

"Right. And our own government is trying to confuse and baffle us so we'll just give up and not even apply. So I have to ask you, Mr. Brainert, have you written about that?"

"Let him answer," someone shouted. "Yes or no?"

"No," he said heavily.

"Did you write about my neighbor, Bella Fishkin, a sweetheart and a darling, with a heart of 22-carat gold who never hurt a fly in her whole life?" asked a woman who so far hadn't made a peep. "When she died, you know what they found in her refrigerator? Purina Cat Chow. But she didn't keep no cat." The group gasped. This was a fear that really hit home. "Kibble or Cumeden, Mr. Brainert, an unholy choice, don't you agree?"

"I'm sorry," the reporter said. "I didn't know."

"That's the whole problem, right there," someone else said. "You didn't know because you didn't ask. Not who, not when, not where, not what and not how." There was a rumble of consent. "Even now he's not asking."

"Didn't I say he was a lazy bum? I said it from the get-go."

"What's the matter, you can't take a bus or a subway like everyone else, maybe ride uptown once and a while?"

"They don't have news in Spanish Harlem or Washington Heights?"

"Please, last time I counted there were four other boroughs."

"What's next? Dispatches from your living room?"

That blow landed squarely and he sat back down looking truly pained, and though I hung my head because of the bad manners, to myself anyway, I couldn't pretend that Joseph and I hadn't made similar comments in the privacy of our Sunday morning *Times* reading ritual.

"Hey, chicky, you take requests?" Mr. Plotsky asked the pianist who was busy sending a text message that probably read: SOS.

She looked to Joseph for guidance.

"One song, Mr. Plotsky." Joseph said. "Your first and your last, so make it count. This is not a...a..." Joseph turned to me for help.

"Talent show?" I offered.

"Karaoke bar," he said definitively.

"Excuse me, but if she had a living relative, why is the shiva here?" Mr. Brainert asked, trying to reassert his rights as a practicing member of the Fourth Estate.

"Why indeed?" I echoed.

"That's what I was wondering too," one of Mrs. Plotsky's girlfriends said, wrapping a heaping plate with a large, crinkled piece of Saran Wrap she'd obviously brought from home in the pocket of her housedress. "Anyways, didn't you call the police on her when you first moved in?"

"What police? You called the Cossacks on an old woman?" the man who'd sounded the alarum against Brainert now spat at me.

Sad to say, while Mrs. Plotsky had been alive, I hadn't really liked her. I hadn't been able to see past what now seemed like minor flaws—the general uncleanliness, the pathological cheapness, not to mention the volume on her television. Did I want to call the police on an old woman who at that time was living alone? No. Did I enjoy hearing the police knock, bang, and ultimately pound on her door because she was so deaf she couldn't hear them over the television? Certainly not. Did it feel good to cower behind my door listening to the wretched scene of her saying "Who is it? Who?" over and over again when she finally did come to the door, because in a million years she couldn't understand why the police would be bothering her at 11 o'clock at night? Again, no. Did I relish the look on the policeman's face when he rang my bell afterwards because he wanted to see the face of the citizen actually heartless enough to

make such a call on a helpless, blind, deaf, and dod-
dering old woman? It's my cross to bear. But if it was
the only way my darling Joseph could get a good night's
sleep then so be it, because the number one priority on
the top of my to-do list is to keep him going, at all times
and at any cost, no matter what sacrifices I have to
make personally, and if the result of that policy is that
certain patrolmen in the NYPD think the worse of me,
and let me know in their own subtle way that if they see
a crime being committed, perpetrated is the word he
actually used, perpetrated against my person they will
cross the street, pretending not to see, then I have to
be able to absorb their criticism, no matter how strong,
and keep putting one foot in front of the other.

"Excuse me," I said, and made my way toward the
front door. "Urgent errand."

"Where are you going?" Joseph called after me, truly
baffled, because he knows no one loves a party more than
me. I'm always the first to arrive and the last to leave.

"Over to the gym."

"Why?"

But I just kept walking. The elevator doors opened
and a crowd got off—showgirls, circus clowns and
transvestites, and I hoped upon hope they were going
to Mr. Plotsky's apartment and not mine.

Though the perfume from the newly arrived revelers
hung heavily in the elevator car, I savored the moment
of silence as I descended to go look for Delmar Clayton
in the fitness center. At the entrance, I pushed the but-
tons for my Fitness Center PIN, placed my whole hand
flat on the state-of-the-art sensor pad and heard the
all-important click.

I passed the restrooms reluctantly. The girdle was pressing somewhat painfully against my bladder, but I didn't think I'd be able to get it off without lying back down, and as spotlessly clean as the Maintenance Department keeps the restrooms, it just didn't seem feasible.

Inside, Mr. Clayton was hitting the heavy bag, grunting and sweating as usual, and I leaned against the windowsill to watch him for a while. I wished I'd brought a sweater with me because, when you're not actually working out down there, it can be a little drafty. After unleashing an avalanche of destruction on his imaginary opponent or opponents, he took a break.

"Hi, Fran...hah...ces." Sweat poured off of him as his overtaxed lungs tried to suck in more oxygen.

"Hello, Mr. Clayton. Good form on the right hook." I'd only taken one kickboxing class in my whole life, but I learned enough to throw the nomenclature around without embarrassing myself.

"Thanks...hee... luggage cart...whoo...yesterday." He gave me a big thumbs up.

"Thanks to Esopus Jeremiah's great instructions. What happened to him after they took the oral history, Mr. Clayton? Did he ever gain his freedom?"

He shook his head, held up a hand, went to the water fountain, and drank for what seemed a long time, quenching a mighty thirst. When he came back over, he could speak again in whole sentences.

"No. Esopus was falsely accused of pilfering an extra ration of rancid lard, and was sold to an even crueler master down South." He said this unblinkingly, fluent in catastrophe.

"Sorry I asked. Speaking of false accusations, any inquiries from the FBI about my library account?"

"Possibly—there was a registered letter delivered today, but it came right at closing time and I didn't get a chance to open it."

That, I have to admit, was annoying. Is it that time-consuming to slice open an envelope?

"Oh, should I be worried?" Maybe he gets a lot of registered mail from the government, form letters and notices and such?

"The timing's awfully suspect. Stop by the branch first thing in the a.m., we open at 10, and I'll let you know."

"Thanks. Uh...Mr. Clayton, you ever worry that your educational work on the slaves might be a double-edged sword?"

"How so?"

"Maybe it gives the wrong kind of people, like managing directors, ideas?"

He shook his head and wiped his brow with his shirtsleeve. "Every day, Frances. Every single day. See you tomorrow."

"Bye, sir. Have a good rest of your workout."

Since I'd already been rude by leaving the shiva, what was another few minutes? I went out the back door and slumped down on a bench in our courtyard. "That was not the all-clear I'd been hoping for," I said to the low branches on the mature trees bowing in the evening's breezes. I looked up through the treetops, less full now than at summer's peak, scouring the night sky, such as it is in Manhattan, for heavenly bodies. I squinted to the north, but Polaris, the polestar guiding navigators through inhospitable wilderness and murky, swelling waters did not dot the i made by the water tower on Building Three.

A commotion in the near distance interrupted my stargazing. My pal Frieda was prone, being carried out of our building on a stretcher, one leg elevated, an IV dripping into her forearm, to the *Hatzoloh* ambulance, which is normally parked curbside on the rare occasion when it's not in use. When you live in a NORC, the ambulance is more like a shuttle bus to the ER, and its regularly blaring siren like the striking of a novelty cuckoo clock. I ran alongside the rescuers, my diaphragm straining against Mrs. Plotsky's girdle.

"Frieda, my God, what happened?" I was panting by the end of this short question.

"Rocko bit me! I've been feeding him since he was a baby, his father before him. He sunk his squirrelly teeth right in my ankle and chomped as hard as he could. I think he hit a vein, possibly an artery."

"Did he?" I asked the young medic.

"There's a lot of blood," he confirmed.

"Rocko's got a great story to tell over a couple of acorn steaks and rainwater martinis down at the local squirrel watering hole," Frieda said, hiding her humiliation at this betrayal by her beloved Rocko. "He sure made a fool of his old friend Frieda."

"Maybe it was a love bite?" I offered. "Maybe it wasn't intentional; he could've confused you with an acorn?"

"Do I look like a nut to you? No, don't make excuses for him. The little fucker knew exactly what he was doing."

"I'm so sorry."

"Don't be," she said. "You told me this day was coming. I'll be stronger now."

"You might be rabid," the medic corrected, fearlessly climbing in the back with her.

"True, but stronger," she insisted.

The ambulance doors slammed, the siren sounded, I plugged my ears and watched them speed off.

Almost instantaneously a van pulled up and beeped its horn to get my attention.

"What great luck," the driver said. It was Sal from Ashes to Ashes. "Now I don't have to find parking and you saved me the trip upstairs."

"What are you doing here, Sal?" I asked, confused and slightly frightened at his reappearance so soon.

He pulled a small package out of the back of his van and handed it out through the window.

"Drop off," he said. "We had a lull at the plant, so I was able to accelerate the usual turn-around time."

"So fast! Is this...?"

"Your neighbor."

The package, though light, was upsetting. I feared its contents might still be warm, hot off the press, like a fresh-baked baguette right out of the oven. I didn't want it and tried to give it back. "No, I think not. Can't you give her to her son?"

"I'd love to do it for you, but the pick-up and drop-off signatures have to match. Company policy."

"So you need me to sign for her?" I said, already resigned to another disagreeable technicality.

"At the X," he said pointing to the line on his clipboard where I scratched my name with the dangling pen tied to a string. "Initials here. Thanks." The bus was pulling up so he sped off to get out of the way, toot-tooting his horn by way of saying goodbye.

I considered dropping the package off at the recycling station, knowing some enterprising Cooperator would put it to good use—cat litter, maybe? But I didn't want to get caught on camera doing anything untoward. Seriously, what was I supposed to do with Mrs. Plotsky's ashes, for God's sake? When I got back upstairs I just opened the door to my chaotic front-hall closet and stashed them in my Go Bag, which was becoming a catchall for some very unusual items.

I re-entered an unexpectedly orderly gathering. In my brief absence, Joseph had completely taken control. Everyone had made a nest with their arms and put their heads down for naptime. The only sound was the pleasant buzzing of light snoring. I made my way over to him.

"Where's Mr. Plotsky and his freaky gang?" I whispered.

"I threatened to send them to the principal's office, and they skedaddled." We high-fived, but quietly.

The *Times* reporter heard us whispering and raised his head.

"Felix, no talking. Put your bird back in its nest," Joseph commanded. And he did.

After another moment, he signaled to the pianist to play a little wake-up music. And while she softly played the hymn "Morning Has Broken" everyone reached and stretched, yawned and sighed.

"Bathroom, one at a time please. Wash your hands," Joseph said. "Sadie, you go first. Then Irving. Around this way."

I went into the kitchen and got the baked apples, Arcadia carried the second tray and we placed them on trivets on the buffet.

"Can I have two volunteers to help pass out the baked apples? Thank you Dotty, thank you Sippi. What is it, Manny?"

"I can't eat cooked apples. They give me the gazzz."

Everyone tittered.

"So don't eat them, Manny. You're a grownup. Eat what you want. No one cares what you eat."

Someone popped a finger inside his cheek to make a farting sound, and I could see Joseph thought it was funny too, but he came down hard on the offender. It was one of the Lubovitchers.

"Moishe, how many rules did you just break?"

"Two?" he asked, fluttering his long and wondrously curled eyelashes.

"That's right. Which ones?"

"The first one."

"Which is?"

"*Respect yourself and all others.*"

"What else?"

"Number three: *If you wish to speak, raise your hand.*"

"So you're smart enough to know the rules, but just stupid enough to break them anyway."

"Honey," I whispered. "Take it easy."

"I can't," he whispered back. "You give them an inch and they'll take everything you've got. They think kindness is weakness."

"I'm sorry," Moishe said, and he really seemed like he meant it.

"Don't *tell* me you're sorry. Show it by behaving and following the rules."

The reporter raised his hand.

"Yes, Felix?"

"My pencil broke. Do you have a sharpener?"

"Frances, please give Felix another pencil. Felix, next time, when you're coming to do an interview, don't just bring one pencil, okay? Do we understand each other?"

"Yes. Are we going to sing some more?"

"Would you like to?"

Everyone shook their heads.

"Okay. One more and we'll commence the debate. Does anyone know, if Mrs. Plotsky had a favorite song?"

Hands shot up.

"Sylvia."

"She loved Louis Armstrong."

"All right. Good suggestion." Joseph had a word with the pianist, who flipped through some sheet music. "Let's do it in C. 'Hello Dolly' it is. One, two, one, two, three."

And everyone sang with gusto except for Arcadia, who clapped along happily enough. We did a few verses and I was amazed at how the older guests remembered every word.

"It's in their long-term memories," Joseph explained to me. Joseph is deep into brain development, especially the latest research on how humans learn, which is just starting to have important implications for how teachers teach. It is definitely the pedagogical wave of the future, very much on his mind, and I suspected we might hear more about it before the evening was through.

Just as the group was sounding the final notes in

the big finish, the three Jehovah's Witness ladies, usually so buttoned down, but now disheveled and dressed strangely as if for Halloween, which I know they don't celebrate, staggered in looking like middle-aged rejects from Destiny's Child. Before they explained I knew what must've happened.

"We were in the wrong apartment. We saw a crowd and followed them," said the mild-mannered church lady. "They stripped us and stole our suits."

"Who did?" Felix Brainert asked.

"The transvestites," her co-religionist answered, now wearing only a sturdy bra and a hula skirt.

Without me even asking her to, Arcadia got busy fixing the new guests each a plate and serving them. I was impressed with her initiative, and if she kept it up, I'd have to say that the sky was pretty much the limit with respect to her tip.

The third woman ate a little, her eyes downcast. "Do you have any hot sauce?" she asked. I had to agree with her—the kreplach *were* on the dull side.

"Louisiana Devil," I answered.

"That will be fine," she said with characteristic dignity.

"Don't worry," Joseph said. "We'll get your clothes back before you leave. Actually, you came just in time. We're about to commence with the main event. A debate, if you will, between me, representing the most evolved ideas of human thought, and you and the Chabad, representing the outmoded Judeo-Christian belief system holding the minds and spirits of this nation hostage. As a matter of fact, Moishe, guys, hello, could I ask you to move your chairs to this side and join the ladies."

Poor Mr. Brainert was writing as fast as he could.

When the Hasids rose to move their chairs, we lost about half of the guests, but that was to be expected. Some had multiple medications to take, favorite TV shows to watch, and one woman hadn't worn her hearing aid, so what was the point?

"Where you going, Rose?" Manny asked the lady who was taking home leftovers. "It's early yet."

"They're starting with the speeches now. I had a nosh, we sang a little. That's enough for me. Lana would understand. But we'll meet again and soon; Isadore from the P building got taken off life support. I'm sad to say, but it shouldn't be long now."

I told Arcadia she could start the washing up if she wanted to get a jump on it. Up to her.

"No, I listen." And she took a seat in the first row. Everyone shifted around and got more comfortable. I cracked a window and cleared some plates while people were settling back down. Mr. Brainert followed me into the kitchen. Feigning a professional cool, he didn't say anything, but his eyes lit up at the sight of the Stellar Marine Silestone countertops and his fingers involuntarily stroked the lacquer cabinetry.

"Mrs. Plotsky must've been extraordinary."

"Yes. She radiated...uh, strength."

"I was struck by the symbol of the girdle on her shiva notice. Can you tell me more?"

Now it was my turn to pull something out of long-term memory. "In Greek mythology, the Amazon Queen wore a golden girdle."

"What was her name?"

"Hip...Hippo...Hippolyte," I joked. And I spelled it for

him. "And Mrs. Plotsky was a leader too, though not regal. She was a woman of the people. She hated the excesses of the overfed, worked her entire adult life to rein them in."

"Can you give me any examples?"

"Yes," I said, thinking of what Delmar Clayton had told me about his meeting with Mrs. Plotsky when she peed on him in the elevator. "She disdained the Nike corporation. She took direct action to take the luster off the brand. Her methods were very successful."

"Thanks. May I quote you?"

"Certainly." I spelled my name for him too. "And if you need a picture, I'm also happy to oblige."

"Okay, folks, let's begin," Joseph said in the living room, loudly enough for us to hear in the kitchen.

"Sorry, I need to get back. I don't want to miss this."

"Me neither," he admitted. We both hurried in to take our seats.

"The first round is Symbols," Joseph was saying. "Okay, let's start with the Jehovah's Witnesses."

They huddled for a moment, and then the one wearing a full slip with a safety-pinned strap rose to address the audience.

"Our symbol is the watchtower. The better from which to see the End of Days." Short and sweet, but to the point. She sat down to polite applause.

"Moishe?"

"Our symbol is the *shofar,* or the ram's horn. In its sounding, we can hear the Almighty's call urging us to follow His commandments."

The applause was slightly more than polite, but still tepid.

"The secular humanist symbol," Joseph said, in a sonorous voice, "is Maslow's pyramid of human needs." He drew a giant pyramid with his arms in the air. "At the base are physiological needs such as food or water, then safety needs such as security and protection, social needs such as sense of belonging and love, esteem needs such as recognition or status, and finally self-actualization." The applause was enthusiastic and I couldn't help letting out a whoop, though I paid the price with a sharp pinch to the waistline.

"The next category is Celebrities," Joseph announced. "Ladies?"

Again they put their heads together, and again the woman in the slip, obviously the delegated spokeswoman, rose to give the team's answer.

"Professional tennis sensations Serena and Venus Williams."

There were a lot of tennis fans in the audience and the response was strong, but the Chabad guys were chomping at the bit.

"At our annual telethon, broadcast from Los Angeles, we've had Academy Award Winners such as Jon Voigt and once even the entire cast of the television show *Friends*."

I heard an approving ripple of "Rachel" and "Chandler" but on balance, the applause was about equal. Joseph let it die down completely. Then he stood and searched the audience's eyes with a penetrating gaze.

"Sports and entertainment are wonderful diversions," he allowed, with a rhetorical flourish, "but did you know that one of the signatories to the 1980 Secular Humanist Declaration was Francis Crick, a Nobel prize winner for co-discovering the structure of the DNA molecule?"

I had no idea the double-helix was such a crowd pleaser, but the response was overwhelming.

"Your husband's wiping the floor with them," Felix Brainert whispered in my ear, leaning in close so the others wouldn't think he was biased.

"Six against one," I said, bursting with pride, "and he hasn't even broken a sweat."

"Before proceeding to the final category, we'll take a few questions from the audience," Joseph announced and hands shot up.

"This is for the Jehovah's Witnesses," said the only Chinese person in the gathering, a woman I've seen digging up plants from the grounds at Seward Park and putting them in a FineFare bag to take home. "If your religion was a food, what it would be?"

"Great question," Joseph said. "Ladies, take your time. No rush."

The pianist filled in the silence while they deliberated with a few tinkling bars of "These are a Few of My Favorite Things." Some heads swayed in time.

"We're ready," the spokeswoman said rising. "If our religion were a food it would be mueslix."

There were a few ooohs and ahhhhs, followed by a good amount of clapping.

"I have a question for the Chabad," said an elderly man I often see sitting in the courtyard reading *The Forward*. "When you guys are parked in the Messiah Mobile, why do you leave the engine idling? Haven't you heard about global warming?"

"That's a no-brainer," Moishe said. "We hope the Messiah will show his face before the melting of the polar ice caps."

"Oh yeah, well let me tell you something, I live on the first floor and the fumes come right in my window. So you're not surprised, I'm telling you now, next time you do it, I'm calling 311."

"The final category is Core Beliefs," Joseph interjected before the Q & A devolved into a free-for-all. "Answers should be judged for clarity and brevity. Ladies, are you ready to make a statement?"

"In a nutshell, we believe that the Bible is the word of God, and when we say Bible, we mean both the Hebrew scriptures and what is commonly referred to as the New Testament. We firmly believe that all of the prophecies written in the Bible—the good, the bad, and the apocalyptic—shall come to pass, and that we must embrace the inevitable and prepare ourselves accordingly. Before I take my seat, I'd like to thank you for your kind attention and mention that we do have some literature. It's free, we brought a lot, and we'd love for you to take it so we don't have to carry it all home."

All three of the Hasids rose, but only Moishe spoke.

"On behalf of the Lubavitch World Headquarters, we also want to thank you. We already gave out our literature, but we have Shabbos candles to distribute. As for the confusion about candle-lighting times," he said, looking in Joseph's direction, "the rule of thumb, for Shabbos anyway, is 18 minutes before sundown."

"Is that Eastern Standard Time?" Sippi asked.

"Why not?" Moishe answered amiably. "If you still have questions, go to the website, www.chabad.org, and click on Ask The Rebbe." One of his colleagues whispered something urgently in his ear. "Also, also, also...I almost forgot, but thanks to Menachem I didn't—our friends at LoHo Realty have asked us to hand out these pens." And he held up a fistful of fat, red plastic pens inscribed with their logo: "LoHo *knows* the Lower East Side."

I could not have been more delighted. Without my even lifting a finger, the party favor issue had completely resolved itself!

"As for core beliefs, I think I can sum it up this way," Moishe continued. "If every day we can get another Jew to do another *mitzvah*, we can accelerate the coming of the Messiah. Why should you care? Because our Rebbe told us, and it's even written on the website, so you can check me on this—'the Messiah will usher in the state of divine goodness and perfection that is the purpose and end-goal of the Almighty's creation.' So I think we can all agree, having the Messiah on the team wouldn't be half bad."

Heads were nodding. Who could say no to a Messianic Age, especially when they're throwing in free candles and pens?

"Candle lighting, *shofar* blowing, dietary laws," Joseph was now saying, "are relics from the past. Strict adherence to ancient texts accumulated before the advent of science and the age of reason simply do not wash in modern times. Rituals and ceremonies, even with sacred intent, are just so many spells and incantations to soothe and falsely console the practitioners. You might as well stir a few newts and toads in a bubbling cauldron and hope for the best. What matters my friends, and what secular humanism is all about," and here he paused for effect, "is the development of each individual to his or her full potential. I leave you with three words: reason, ethics, and justice."

Arcadia was fascinated. I, too, was spellbound. There was a moment's hesitation while the crowd waited to make sure Joseph was done speaking and then a thunderous ovation exploded, filling the living room. Mr. Brainert was up on his feet to pump Joseph's hand, the clear winner in the battle of ideas.

"He'd be good speaker for the next NORC luncheon," Sippi said to her friend Dotty as she rocked back and forth on the couch to get some momentum going before lift off.

"Ask his wife first," Dotty said. "She'll get him to do it."

I smiled at the compliment.

The guests thanked the panelists before they filed out, and I noticed the Jehovah's Witnesses were getting a lot of positive feedback on the meuslix answer. They left in a warm tangle of Cooperators, content to retrieve their outfits another day, and I hoped for their sakes that the wind had died down.

On the way out, one of the Hasids asked another, "So, who was this Maslow character with his human needs? I never heard of him. Was he by any chance Jewish?"

Joseph and Felix Brainert were deep in a conversation about brain development that segued into a discussion about multiple intelligences, so Arcadia and I headed for the kitchen. I was pleased to see there were no leftovers to speak of. I'd ordered just the right amount of food, not too much, not too little. For the cleanup, I poured a nice long shot of Calvados in a mug of cider and offered the same to Arcadia, but she refused.

"Alright, *mi amiga*. You don't know what you're missing," I said, as the first sip warmed my chest.

After a few minutes of loading what we could in the dishwasher and organizing the rest, I wandered back into the living room, where the pianist was all packed up. While settling with her, I asked her how she was planning on getting home.

"I'll just catch a cab," she said, without a trace of tiredness on her angelic face. "I still have a couple of hours of practicing ahead of me. Some tricky partitas, and I have to keep at it."

"I'd better call you a car service. More reliable at this hour." And I called New Day and asked for a safe driver with a clean driving record and a nice, non-smoking car. "They said three minutes. In front of the bus stop. Need help?"

"No. I can manage."

I interrupted Joseph to tell him the pianist was leaving.

"Bye Sasha," he said, embracing her in a big bear hug. "Let us know about your next recital, okay?" She was beaming.

Felix Brainert offered to walk her downstairs and we all said our goodbyes.

Joseph pitched in with the cleanup, mostly taking a few loads of trash to the chute and repositioning the furniture where it belonged, and with all three of us working together, we were finished in no time. We walked Arcadia to the door.

"I couldn't have done it without you, Arcadia. Thank you so much." I handed her the fee plus a generous tip. "And on such short notice too."

"It's too much," she protested when she saw the little wad of cash I'd pressed in her hand.

"You deserve it," Joseph said. "Every time I looked out in the audience, you were smiling. It was very encouraging. How're you getting home? *A casa?*"

"I walk."

"What? No," he said, looking at me.

"Honey, she lives right here on Pitt Street. Pitt and Broome, isn't it?"

She nodded. "I okay. Bye."

"See you next Thursday," I said as always, and closed and locked the door.

"Come here, you little sexual humanist," Joseph said, pulling me close. "You've been driving me crazy all night."

"You were great," I said as he covered my neck with kisses. "You were so animated, such a good public speaker. I was so proud to know you, much less be married to you."

"Why thank you," he said, pulling my top off over my head. He was reaching for the back of my bra when the doorbell rang. "Don't answer it," he whispered feverishly.

"Maybe somebody forgot something, honey. I have to," I said, pulling my top back on and smoothing it down. When I looked through the peephole I was surprised to see the lovely retarded woman. I opened the door about halfway. "Yes, dear?"

"I'm here for the shiva," she said in her flat drone, her whole face smiling. I looked at Joseph behind the door who was making shooing motions like I was supposed to send her away. But I couldn't. I just couldn't.

"Please come in," I said. "Sit down, dear. What can I get you? Do you like rugelach? Some hot apple cider?"

She nodded.

"This is a nice place! The river looks so...shiny." The bursting moon was bathing the inky waves in ivory light.

"Thank you. I'll be right back." Joseph said a quick hello and followed me in the kitchen while I got her snack. "She'll be here fifteen minutes, twenty tops."

"I'm gonna take a shower," he said. "I'll be waiting for you." He kissed me and patted me on my behind while I poured myself a half a shot more of Calvados. When I got back to the living room with a small tray, the lovely retarded woman was crying. I sat down next to her and handed her a steaming mug, suppressing the urge to blow on it for her.

"Mrs. Plotsky was nice to me. I feel sad she died."

"I know you saw her every day. Were you close with her?"

"She scratched my back. I got one place where it's real itchy, and she used to scratch it."

"That is nice."

"Yeah. This is good," she said about the cider. "I like Stanley too. He's funny."

I wondered if he was going to drop her, now that he had found a new crowd courtesy of Craig's List.

I yawned. "Sorry, it's been a long day."

"Are you tired?" she asked me, and put the mug down to make a sleepy sign with both hands pressed together against her face.

"I am. You?"

"I'm a night person. An owl. Whooo. Whooo."

We both laughed. I glanced at my watch and saw that only two of the twenty minutes I'd allotted had passed. Inspiration struck.

"I was just going to play a game," I said, moving toward the desk and getting the Dolch labels and index cards. "It's easy. You just take the label off and put it as neatly as you can in the middle of the index card. Like this."

And then she did one. "I like stickers," she said.

Whatever her other problems might have been, her fine motor skills were unimpaired and we worked together until the three remaining Dolch sets were completed.

"Did I win?" she asked me as I bagged the new sets.

"Yes."

"Is there a prize?" she asked, her broad face already lighting up with joy.

"Of course. The winner gets a prize." And I opened a curio cabinet and took out a slender kaleidoscope I'd bought in a museum gift shop maybe 25 years ago, a lead pipe with two stained glass pinwheels at the end, each the size of a silver dollar but a quarter of an inch thick. I showed her how to aim it at a light source, look through the hole and manipulate the wheels, both in the same direction, in opposite directions, fast, slow, and spinning with abandon.

"Beautiful," she said. "*Beautiful*. BEAUTIFUL. For me?"

"For you."

She put her arms up in the air in a "v" for victory.

I walked her out to the elevator and waved as the doors were closing. As I turned the corner, one of Mr. Plotsky's guests opened his apartment door to leave. As he breezed by with an unopened bottle of champagne tucked under his arm, a fragrant gust of marijuana wafted out. Maybe it was mixed with hashish? For the first time in four years I breathed deeply near the Plotskys' door.

Peering through the smoky gray haze, I saw one of the transvestites, tall, with a ballerina's arms, sitting on the wretched sofa. Her light brown hair was long and lank over her shoulders, and her powdered face seemed chiseled from marble. Across her lap lay the pillowy torso of a spent Mr. Plotsky. Talk about your bathetic Pietà in *tableau vivant*.

Back in my apartment, I kicked off my pumps and started stripping off my clothes as I made my way to the bedroom, where understandably, my husband was snoring. Stymied by the girdle, I tugged with all my might, but it was even more of a struggle to pull off than it was to get on. Desperate, I retrieved the kitchen shears from their drawer, but the sharp teeth couldn't make a dent in the industrial-strength fabric, and I went back to the slow process of inching it down my abdomen. While trying to wriggle out of it without performing a bellybuttonectomy, I looked at the clock—11:45 p.m. In just six hours he was going to have to start his Friday after a long, hard week, and I had a choice to make. Was I really going to wake him up, as much as I wanted him and needed his arms around me, his mouth on mine, his sweat mingling with my own, wake him up and rouse him to insist on passion? At our age? After all these years together? Was that reasonable?

Another Trip to the Library

I awoke with the beginnings of a throbbing stye in my right eye—not from sex with my husband, which I don't discuss, unless there's a medical reason and only then with a medical professional—but in my rush to carnal pleasure I'd neglected to remove my eye makeup. Mascara, shadow, and liner melted into my eyeball in a petroleum by-product slime of Exxon Valdez proportions, occluding God knows what. I was making a hot compress when it dawned on me, incredibly, that it was 7:30 a.m., not the usual indecent wake-up time of 5:45 a.m., that Joseph had already left for work, and I was alone in the apartment. Without my assistance, words of encouragement, or even a kiss goodbye, he'd gotten up, dressed, and out. I felt positively unmoored.

I made some coffee and, while it brewed, tended to

my sore eye, hoping upon hope I could heat-blast the swarming bacteria into remission and it would not develop into the full-blown deforming mess it was yearning to become.

With hot coffee in one hand and hot compress in the other, I wandered into the living room. The beauty of the all-white bouquet on the black credenza stopped me in my tracks. Having been cut and harvested, the flowers were, of course, themselves dying, but for the moment the petals still held firm to the blooms, and the scent was not yet reminiscent of low-lying swamps and flooded basements. The arrangement of stalks, leaves, and blossoms in various stages of unfolding, from tight buds to already ruinously splayed, was a still-life meditation on the natural life cycle, with its in-your-face fecundity and promise of imminent decay.

As heavy as it was, I hauled the vase into the kitchen and set it in the sink to dump out yesterday's cloudy water and replace it with fresh. I threw in an aspirin, so they'd last and last, and while I had the childproof bottle cap open, popped a couple down the hatch myself.

Tacked on a rose thorn, the little cream-colored envelope from my florist was still unopened, so I pulled out the matching card and read, with my good left eye, the message that filled it, written in teensy, neat handwriting:

> For she's a jolly good fellow, for she's a jolly good
>   fellow
> For she's a jolly good fellow, which nobody can
>   deny
> Which nobody can deny, which nobody can deny

For she's a jolly good fellow, for she's a jolly good
    fellow
For she's a jolly good fellow, which nobody can
    deny

I had only one minor quibble with the florist's card, whose message I was growing to endorse now that I was getting to know more about my former neighbor. And that was the tense. Properly, shouldn't it have somehow indicated that Mrs. Plotsky was in the past a jolly good fellow? Because now, her cremated ashes and bone shards sat in a most unjolly machine-wrapped, brown paper package tied with a length of string in my Go Bag. Mrs. Plotsky was and is no more. Long live Mrs. Plotsky.

The phone rang and it was Joseph.

"Hi tiger," I said. "Thanks for letting me sleep in."

"You were snoring so hard, I didn't have the heart to wake you."

"*I* was snoring?"

"Like a leaf blower. That was a lot of fun last night."

"What was?"

"The shiva, the sex, all of it."

"Do me a favor and don't link them in your mind," I said, turning the compress over for a little more heat.

"Very funny. Are we sitting tonight?"

"Not supposed to on Friday night. The Sabbath."

"What about Saturday?"

"Opera tickets."

"Sunday?"

"I don't think so, honey. You need time to do your paperwork for school."

"Sounds like that was it. We built the bench for a single night?"

"I'm afraid so. We'll go in and out on the same high note."

"I can't wait to see the City section on Sunday. We'll be immortalized!"

We both laughed.

"Doing anything special with the kids today?"

"Teaching a new song. Some of them are having difficulty memorizing the Pledge of Allegiance, so I put it to music."

"Brilliant. Play it for me tonight?"

"Sure. I wrote a crescendo at the end. *With liberty and justice FOR ALL.* I hope they really sing out." I heard a long clanging bell. "Gotta run," he said, rushing off.

"Bye," I said to the ether.

Ether made me think of cyber and I powered on the computer to finally check the Co-op Village Online Message Board as I'd promised Josh I would do, and as I very much wanted to do—but the message board no longer existed!

I e-mailed Josh Dishkin immediately. "Josh, what gives? Tried to read recent posts, especially on the thread I started and I got a screen saying our community no longer exists. Huh???"

He responded immediately.

"It's true. The upshot of your post was a consensus that we were too disembodied and too focused on minutiae when there were true crises taking place under our noses. We're going to start meeting in person regularly and sharing information the old-fashioned way. Person to person."

I wrote back.

"You mean get dressed and leave the house? No more hiding behind anonymity? Real engagement with human beings?"

"Yes," he answered. "We won't have the same level of anti-virus protection, but it's a chance most of us are willing to take. Our first meeting's tonight at Full City. Mention the former message board to receive a 10% discount on cappucinos and herbal teas."

"Thanks, buddy. I'll try and stop by."

That gave me something to think about during my aqua-torture drills. Even in Cooperative Village, when change finally happens, it comes fast and forever. I filled the bath, gathered my equipment, and got to work.

Submerging my head under the hot water felt good on my aching eye, and I was able to achieve some positive results on multiple fronts. My scores were in a steady upward trajectory, but I had to stop when someone insistently rang my doorbell.

I got out, threw Joseph's thick bathrobe on, and padded to the front door.

"Who is it?" I called, before peeping.

"Home ke-yah," the voice called out in a broad Massachusetts accent. It was a NINNY home-care nurse! Mostly brawny women, they're local heroes who charge into the trenches every day, going into smelly apartments to perform wound and every other kind of care for my neighbors who need and deserve it. This ruddy number looked like she'd be most at home wearing denim overalls, milking a cow with one hand and fixing the tractor with the other, which I mean as a compliment. She seemed capable. I opened the door and poked my dripping head out.

"Never met a nurse I didn't like. How are you?" I asked, trying to tamp down the fight-or-flight adrenaline reaction at seeing the NINNY logo embroidered on her shirt, pants, rolling backpack, and stamped on her pen. I flashed on a horrible vision of the managing director with a red-hot branding iron in hand, laughing a maniacal laugh, and his entire Executive Leadership Cabal lined up on all fours with their pants down, the smell of their colleagues' seared flesh already stinking up the conference room.

"Mrs. Plotsky?" she asked, reading the name off a clipboard also emblazoned with the NINNY insignia.

"What? Oh no." I laughed at her comical error. Imagine someone mistaking me for Mrs. Plotsky.

"I was scheduled to see a Mrs. Plotsky today," she said, getting right down to business.

"The other door, over there. But do yourself a favor and knock, don't ring." And I started to close the door.

"I tried there first. A man, at least I think it was a man, said he no longer knew anyone by that name. Told me to try here."

I described Mr. Plotsky.

"That's him," she confirmed. "He said if she's anywhere on earth, she'd probably be at your house."

"For the record, that's one of her sons. Okay. Let me get her for you. Just a moment, please." And I retrieved the package from my Go Bag in the closet and handed it out to her.

"There goes my George Foreman grill," the nurse said, examining the box with the Ashes to Ashes label. "And I was this close." She held up her fingers to indicate half an inch.

"What're you talking about?"

"Just the best darned sales contest our managing director has ever announced. To incentivize the sales force...I mean clinicians." And here she pulled out a very handsome laminated sheet detailing the prizes available. The dishwasher-safe grills were at the first rung, but the premiums went all the way up to an all-expenses-paid, six-nights, seven-day trip to Bermuda, with a welcoming afternoon tea and complimentary cricket match. "And Mrs. Plotsky sounded like a great prospect."

"Better luck next month. Just curious, how do you identify your prospects?"

"Business Development generates lists. Between you, me, and the fire extinguisher over there, they're not worth the paper they're printed on. Mostly, I schmooze with the locals at the NORC. That means to talk informally."

"Please, I know what schmooze means."

"From what they told me about Mrs. Plotsky, I was going to be able to refer her for physical therapy, occupational therapy, speech therapy, down the road maybe hospice—I had a whole list. But it looks like I'm a day late and a dollar short."

"Mrs. Plotsky didn't need speech therapy."

"Really? Are you a credentialed professional? Qualified to make that assessment, are you?" Her eyes narrowed and any trace of a smile was wiped from her no-non-sense face.

"She doesn't need it now. Surely you can see that?"

She nodded, only half-listening.

"Can I put you down for some grief counselling? I

could have a certified hospice doula stop by within 24 hours. If you book services today, I can throw in an author-signed copy of *Chicken Soup for the Soul*. That's the hardcover."

"No thanks. We're good. I'm already under a mental health professional's care, and my husband seems to be taking her passing in stride."

"Okay," she said, handing me back Mrs. Plotsky's ashy remains. "While I'm here, I could take a look at that eye. Are you Medicaid-eligible by any chance?"

"No. No thank you. It's just a stye."

I watched her make some notes on her computer notebook. Even upside down I could read: "Examined patient. Seemed to be in a deteriorated condition. Felt for pulse—none. Blood pressure—none. Reflexes—none. Pain level 1–10. Zero." She received a pop-up alert on her screen that prompted her to follow certain accepted protocols.

"Next time, don't use Ashes to Ashes." And she handed me a coupon. "We have an in-house crematorium. It's the Gold Standard in high-temperature pulverizing."

I shuddered. Can Soylent Green protein pellets be far behind?

"Before I go," she asked, "could you use a refrigerator magnet with our toll-free number? All you have to do is take a brief customer-service survey."

"I've got the Kenmore Elite with the stainless finish and I don't like the clutter." Normally I would've invited her in to see the kitchen, but no one voluntarily wearing a NINNY logo crosses my threshold. "But do you have one of those little rubber jar lid twist-off things? Those are very handy." And you can scrape the logo off with a butter knife. I know because that's what I did with my last one.

"Let me look in my bag." And she pulled out a miniature sewing kit, a BandAid dispenser, and a 7-day plastic pill case. "Want a couple of these instead?"

"No. If you have the jar opener I'll take that, otherwise, I'll just get back to my morning bath," I said, starting to shut the door, but she stuck her foot against it.

"Just to be on the safe side, you really should have someone take a look at that eye. It could be a Cochdablochtafloria."

"A cochdablochta what?"

"Infectious, and highly contagious, in which case I'd have to alert the Department of Health and get the ball rolling for quarantine."

"What?! What did you just say? Quarantine? Are you threatening me in my own home?"

"I have the public health to think about," she hissed, holding up her cell phone, her now-wild eyeballs spinning in their sockets. "I've got Commissioner Frieden's telephone number on my speed-dial."

"Put that down a minute. Listen to me. Believe me, I know you're under a lot of pressure to make your productivity targets, but don't you think you're coming on a wee bit strong for a free kitchen appliance? You nurses make a good living. If you want a grill so badly, why not take the M22 bus to J&R and buy one? Buy two. Buy three! Why degrade yourself like this? You're a registered nurse for God's sake. The good you do in one shift, they can't do in a lifetime of number crunching. Don't let them turn you into a Fuller Brush man. And isn't there still a nursing shortage in this country?

My God woman, you're in the driver's seat. If you think NINNY should give you a free 'lean, mean, fat grilling machine,' march into the VP of Human Resources's office and demand one. They'll find a way to justify it. It's what they do best. Now c'mon. Take your foot off my doorjam and get a grip on yourself."

Somewhere around Fuller Brush man her face had collapsed and the inevitible bawling began. I just let her sniffle and weep because sometimes a person needs to feel pain in order to make an important change.

"I'm so sorry," she finally said through her tears. "They push and they push and this is what happens. Since I started working at NINNY, I don't recognize myself. Forgive me."

"I do. Of course I do. I'm sure the real you would've been very kind to Mrs. Plotsky, and that means a lot."

"Have you got a tissue?" she asked me. "Please?"

"Sure. Hold on." I brought the Kleenex box back to the door. "Help yourself. Take as many as you need. Take a few more for later, for when you break down again."

"Thanks. Thank you," she said, blowing her nose, making an unattractive honking sound. A little snot escaped the tissue and sprayed onto her shirt landing on the embroidered NINNY logo, but I didn't say anything. She's a nurse. What's a little mucus to her? Besides, if anyone saw it they wouldn't necessarily assume it was her snot.

I helped her gather up her equipment.

"Listen, I might know of an opportunity for you. My neighbor, over there in the corner. Maybe, mind you there's no guarantees, and you didn't hear it from me, but she might need a flu shot. I know she likes to get them early. It's something of a point of pride with her."

"I have some serum with me! Which door?" she asked starting to move in the direction I'd pointed in.

"09. Also, you could check the battery on her hearing aid. She might need a replacement. I heard something chirping, could be her smoke alarm. You're the RN; you'll figure it out."

"Thank you," she said. "Thanks for everything."

"You're welcome. And thank you, too, for taking the healing to my house, or, you know, trying to."

Now I really had to get a move on if I was going to arrive at the scheduled time to meet Mr. Clayton at the library and receive the verdict in the case of The Government of the United States of America v. Me. Before I left, I quickly dressed and I tidied up a bit, putting Mrs. Plotsky's ashes back in the Go Bag. I listened at Mr. Plotsky's door to hear if he was all right, or if the loss of his mother had hit him with its full force as I expected it soon would. But all I could hear was the television, on lower than usual, and the pleasant hum of someone vacuuming the living room.

On my way to the library I stopped off at each of the four buildings to pull down the shiva notices I'd posted—was it just yesterday?—noting the new ones, none of whom, thankfully, I recognized. A few copycats had also featured underwear of the deceased on their shiva notices, and I was flattered. There was one with a pair of rumpled, dirty socks I found particularly poignant.

For the third day in a row, the weather was unbeatable, sunshine and blue skies that felt like a benediction. A lot of Cooperators were already out, and I scanned the parks for Frieda, hoping she'd been successfully discharged from the ER after her contretemps with Rocko. Retracing my steps to the library, I also searched the horizon for my friend, whose name I did not know, to see if he was outside the Masaryk Convenience Store. He wasn't around, which was a shame, because I wanted to tell him about the community meeting at Full City. Not only because the more the merrier, but he could add a lot to the forum as a neighbor from Bernard Baruch housing and as, you know, an ex-felon.

I arrived a moment or two early at the Hamilton Fish branch and waited on the sidewalk for the staff to open the doors, becoming more and more nervous with each passing second at the prospect of getting bad news.

"Finally!" I accidentally said out loud, drawing the ire of the guard who unlocked the door. I started at the sight of the usually girly security guard, whose pants were now stuffed into tall black leather boots. Her fingernails were long and decorated with gilt polish, but her beaded braids were tucked under a green felt beret. She in turn gave me the once over, staring at my shirt, which I now saw I'd buttoned askew in my hurry.

"At least it's not inside out," I joked, fixing it quickly and dropping my keys noisily on the sidewalk in the process.

When I stood up again, she was not smiling.

"Slowly, keeping your hands where I can see them at all times, let me see your library card," she demanded.

"I...I don't have it on me. Last time I was here the librarian canceled my card. My entire account's been closed until further notice." Her eyes contracted to pinholes. "It wasn't my fault," I added too late.

"What's your purpose in coming to the library today?"

I was self-conscious about my swollen eyelid and, given the circumstances, defensive and perhaps a little paranoid. I shifted back and forth nervously before responding and lost my footing, stumbling and just catching myself against the wall.

"Weak ankles," I explained. "Never much of an ice skater."

"I'm going to ask you again, ma'am, why are you here?"

"The FBI might be after me," I whispered. "Not that it's any of your concern, but if it happened to me it could happen to you."

"Sorry, ma'am," she said, pulling me to the side. "I'm going to need to ask you to take a Breathalyzer test."

"Why? If anything, I drank too much coffee this morning. Maybe it made me a little jittery, but I'm not high."

"Then the test should come out all right." She handed me a balloon. "Blow into this, please."

A few other patrons were filing into the library now, going through the turnstile, looking at me with a mixture of pity and disgust.

"Look, I have an appointment with Mr. Delmar. He's expecting me. I mean Dr. Clayton. Why don't we go inside and ask him together?"

"Why don't you do as I ask and blow into the balloon?"

"I'm not drunk," I said, probably a little too loudly, because someone shushed me from inside. "Let me walk a straight line or touch my nose," I said in a quieter voice. "I'll prove it to you."

"Ma'am, please, blow."

So I stood on the wrong side of the turnstile blowing into a balloon, simultaneously furious and humiliated.

"That's enough," she said, when I got it about half-filled. But I didn't stop. Oh no. I kept blowing and blowing, her round brown eyes in her dark face getting bigger and bigger as the balloon inflated, stretching beyond reason and finally popping sharply, like a gunshot.

"Oops."

"Think you're a wise guy, huh." She reached around to her back pocket, pulled out a Taser, and lunged for me.

Bobbing, weaving, and barely escaping, I screamed bloody murder.

"Mr. Clayton! MIS-TER CLAY-TON, help me! Stop her!!!" He came rushing out, a suave savior in wide-wale corduroy and herringbone tweed.

"What's going on here?" he demanded, his shock at the fracas plainly distorting his normally placid, if rubbery face.

"This woman is trying to stun me!" I cried.

"Dora-May, take it easy. I know Frances. She's a longtime library patron. Always returns her books on time, sometimes well before the due date." Still agitated, she continued waving her arms around. "Now, come on, before you accidentally hurt someone." Gently, he put his hand on her arm to calm her down. "I can vouch for her. Take a walk around the block. Go on. Don't come back until you're over it."

Since he was the Branch Manager, and a superior officer in the chain of command, she had no choice but to let me pass under his protection.

"I'm sorry about that," he said, as he walked me over to the desk out on the library floor, not the one in his personal office behind closed doors. "She's just come back from a training seminar at the Office of Emergency Management and they've got her all hepped up."

"Let's hope it's temporary. She was getting ready to neutralize me. Why does a library guard need to be armed? Don't you find that ominous?"

"These are the new regulations. Like everyone else, I have to find a way to live with them." He arranged his stapler and paperclip holder on his desk, and then switched their positions, avoiding my eyes. "I see you're *sola* today, Frances," he said, changing the unpleasant subject.

"Yes sir," I said, as my speedy heart rate returned to something approaching normal.

"Mrs. Plotsky's been dispatched to her final resting place I take it?"

"Mezzo-mezzo," I answered. "The cremation's behind her, but her ashes are stashed in my front closet until inspiration strikes."

"Well, I heard you gave her a grand send-off. I did a load of laundry this morning, and everyone, and I mean everyone, was whistling show tunes. I'm sorry to have missed it. It sounded like a gay evening."

"That's okay, Mr. Clayton. Next time. Did you get a chance to open the envelope from the Federal Bureau of Investigation?"

"I did and I'm very sorry to tell you—" But he couldn't finish his sentence because a patron standing behind me had an urgent question. "Good morning, Mr. Abrahamson," Mr. Clayton greeted him. The name sounded familiar. "What can I do for you today?"

"I see you're busy, so I'll get right to the point. My wife was at some kind of lecture last night, refreshments they served, kreplach even they had, don't ask. When she came home she couldn't stop talking about meuslix, a joker named Maslow and some kind of pyramid. I asked her for details, so for once we could have an interesting discussion, instead of her usual kvetching, but she couldn't remember what the pyramid was for."

"Oh, I think I might know—"

"—Excuse me, but *I'm* talking now. So then I thought, maybe it's the food groups? Do you have such a book, maybe by a nutritionist named Dr. Maslow?"

"Give me a moment," Mr. Clayton said to me.

"Sure." And while he sorted out Mr. Abrahamson's request, I let my thoughts drift. What was I, in fact, going to do with Mrs. Plotsky's ashes? Fling them from the pedestrian walkway on the Williamsburg Bridge? It's a possibility, and one I'd probably enjoy, but only if the wind was blowing the right way. Take them down to the river bank and let the currents wash her out to the Long Island Sound? Lovely in theory, but people fish right there. Sprinkle them in the gardens at Corlear's Hook Park? Owners bring their dogs to pee and worse there. Leave the package on the F train and let her ride the rails to glory? I like the folksiness, but because of the MTA's relentless "If You See Something, Say Something" program, it would probably be reported as suspicious before she made it out to Coney Island.

Mr. Clayton came back, took his seat, and resumed our meeting.

"As I was saying, the letter was, as we'd feared, a

formal request to turn over your library record. I have no choice but to comply. It's the law of the land."

"The so-called Patriot Act."

"The Uniting and Strengthening America by Providing Appropriate Tools Required to Intercept and Obstruct Terrorism Act of 2001, to be exact. A mouthful, I know."

"Former Attorney General Ashcroft probably stayed up way past his usual bedtime to pen that one, huh?"

Mr. Clayton laughed, which just encouraged me.

"Or, I know, he couldn't work it into the lyrics of his quote-unquote song, 'Let the Eagle Soar,' so he wrote a repressive legislative act instead."

"Ashcroft was a *shmegeggie*," Mr. Abrahamson piped in from over by the Large Type section. "But this new one—they should send him back to where he came from, Sodom *and* Gemorrah. What's the matter with your eye?"

"My eye?"

"It's oozing."

"Is it?" I asked Mr. Clayton. He nodded and handed me a box of tissues. I took a half-a-dozen, one after another and dabbed. "These old Cooperators," I whispered, "you don't know whether to kill them or kiss them. May I see the paperwork, please?"

"Certainly." Mr. Clayton unlocked his desk drawer and handed me the envelope with the raised seal.

The letter was brief and to the point. My name was spelled correctly and my date of birth was right, too, though I wasn't so thrilled about them sharing that information with Mr. Clayton. Torture and degradation aside, don't suspected enemy combatants have any right to privacy at all? What about HIPAA?

The letter was over the signature of FBI Director Robert S. Mueller III, with courtesy copies sent to U.S. Attorney General Gonzales and New York State Assembly Speaker Sheldon Silver. Nice of him to keep them in the loop.

"Damn them! How much time do I have?"

"I don't have much wiggle room. I'll be turning the record over by the end of business on Monday, so you have the weekend's head start. Also, I want to remind you that they may already be listening in on your phone line. So *ix-nay* on the *ome-heh, one-phay*."

"Right." My eye spasmed painfully and I winced.

"Joking aside, are you okay, Frances?"

"Not really, Mr. Clayton. It's no picnic coming under their scrutiny like this just because I happened to have some extra time on my hands and love to read. I'm not looking forward to having to tell my husband, who needs this like a hole in the head. And frankly, there's the un-welcome expense of a costly defense, which can be a lot to bear for a middle-class couple, especially now that we're down to one income—when you count lawyers' fees and factor in the opportunity cost, the numbers can be staggering. Also, I can't help it, I know it's not personal, but it rankles that my taxes fund their more-than-generous salaries, and this is how they choose to repay me. But the very worst part is the anxiety from the uncertainty; once you get embroiled in their video-game fantasies, there's no predicting the outcome. I could do everything perfectly, and still lose my liberty, causing my husband endless heartache in the process. All in all, I've had better days."

Mr. Clayton sighed and I was sorry for dumping on him. "Thank you for your time." And I rose to leave. "You've been wonderful."

"It's no trouble." He stood up to walk me out. "I just wish I could help in some concrete way. There's one thing I can suggest. Do you know any spirituals?"

I was momentarily distracted by Mr. Abrahamson pestering people on the check-out line about their selections.

"Songs? I might remember a few they taught us in elementary school. Why?"

"The African chattel slaves found them to be a comfort as they faced the injustices of their day. Might give you a lift if you're feeling low."

I have to admit this was not such an appealing option. With me and spirituals, a little goes a long way. But I was diplomatic.

"The Jordan River's deep and wide, milk and honey's on the other side."

At the door, I extended my hand for a normal businesslike handshake, but Mr. Clayton did the oddest thing. He curled his fingers in mine and gave me the Black Power handshake instead. And if that wasn't surprising enough, he leaned over, grabbed my forearm, and whispered in my ear: "Power to the people. Right on with your bad self!"

I was so charged up that, right there on Houston Street, I raised my fist in the air and pumped. A couple of drivers tooted their car horns, and pumped their raised fists too. Now *that* gave me a lift.

Outside the library, I immediately began my hunt for a working payphone from which to call Hope, and had to walk all the way back to Grand Street before I found one. I dialed the 718 number I knew so well by heart, and got her machine announcing yet another of her increasingly frequent getaways.

"...law offices of Hope Hardon. If this is an emergency, please leave a detailed message at the tone, otherwise please call back on Tuesday. Thank you." The beep sounded.

"Hi Hope, it's...uh...um...me," I said, trying to be discreet. "Please be in touch, though my ability to speak freely on my home phone may be limited, hence the emergency. Tuesday, however, will probably be too late."

And then while I was thinking about it, I dropped another quarter of Joseph's hard-earned money in the payphone and called 311 to report the gaping pothole on Columbia Street. It wasn't going to fix itself.

10

The Girdle's Last Gasp

When they came for Ethel Rosenberg, she was standing at her kitchen sink washing her dirty lunch dishes, hands wet and soapy. All the more reason I was glad we'd popped for the Kenmore Elite Smart dishwasher, which does everything for you but load and unload itself. Nor have I ever regretted purchasing the extended warranty, pricey as it was. It came in especially handy the single time Joseph loaded the dishwasher, when he neglected to throw away some olive pits before placing a plate inside. Sears had to put in a whole new motor for that one.

The phone rang, interrupting me from polishing my Silestone countertops to a high gloss, tidying up my already tidy kitchen. Given Mr. Clayton's warning about wire-tapping, I reluctantly answered it.

"Hi Frances, it's Serena. How are you? Actually don't

answer that, I've got someone coming in a minute."

"Hi, Serena."

"The reason I'm calling is I have a cancellation this afternoon; we should meet again, and I'd like you to bring your journal. You have been journaling the girdle, haven't you?"

"Journaling the girdle," I repeated, delighted to be confounding the eavesdropping G-men. "Sure. I live for journaling the girdle! What time?"

"One."

It was 11:20 a.m.

"Did you want me to come all the way up there?"

"Yes, in fact I insist upon it. You seem to be building some psychological barrier toward traveling uptown, which I don't have to tell you is extremely unhealthy for a New Yorker. The island's only twelve-and-a-half miles long to begin with. You start carving out whole territories, your world gets awfully small, awfully fast."

"Fine, but I'm not doing the whole make-up, hair, uptown matchy-matchy outfit thing, not on such short notice. And be forewarned, I haven't had time to get a manicure either."

She sighed at the obvious signs of deterioration.

"Just put on some dark glasses and a little bright lipstick. Wear some earrings and tie a silk scarf around your neck. That will signal that you know better, but are taking a pass—every woman's right on occasion, even those of us who are role models with the highest possible standards."

Wow. Was Serena mellowing? Or was this rash of cancellations forcing her to cut her remaining clients some slack?

"Alright, I'll be there. If I leave now, I can just make it in time."

Even though I was basically wearing sneakers, leggings, and a sweatshirt, I followed her accessorizing directions to a tee, decorating my neck and head as a thing wholly apart from my body. I grabbed a hardback journal and a pen from my desk, and retrieved my dusty Metrocard from where it rested unused in recent months, reasoning I could travel by bus, save the cab fare and journal the girdle on the way.

I found the girdle on my closet floor and wriggled back into the blasted thing, grunting and groaning, and wanting to cry real salt tears at the effort. At the last minute, I retrieved a pen with another ink color as well as a pencil, so I could make it look like the entries were written at different times of the day and night, the way it really would be in a true journal, not one falsified at the last possible minute to appease Serena. I locked up tight and headed downstairs for the journey to the other side of 14th Street, one I'd not taken in far, far too long.

Last year, Speaker Silver kindly installed a bench at our bus stop, and I pushed myself right down to start writing while I waited for the M14A driver to finish his break. Our bus stop is both the end of the line and the beginning of the line, depending on how you want to look at it.

I started with the blue ink pen, writing whatever thoughts and feelings occurred to me, censoring nothing no matter how silly or inane.

Like a message, in a bottle, found a girdle just now, I just now found a girdle, from the fifties, just now!

It was smelly, it was stinky, it was stenching,
    right now, oh the girdle was so nasty, was so
    funky, right now.
Wore it anyway, bore it anyway, wore it anyhow
    right now, I just now wore it anyway, damn this
    girdle, right now.

GIRDLE ANAGRAM INTO FREE ASSOCIATION:
Gird, glide, girl, ride, grid, rile, dreg, dire.
Dirigible. Digestible. Comestible. Constable.
Congestion. Confusion. Confession.

Two solid journal entries, and it was time to get on
the bus. Or try to, anyway, because with the girdle con-
stricting my range of hip motion, I couldn't take the
high stairs to board in the usual way. The driver had to
send the elevated platform down to the street for me, as
if I were in a wheelchair, a Jazzy, or had a walker. I felt
encumbered. I felt special. I felt I belonged. I wrote all
the contradictory feelings down, spontaneously captur-
ing them for the journal, and then I changed pens.

Foundation garment from the fifties. I was born
in the fifties. Chance for rebirth? Foundations
tunnel underground. What's in my psychic
basement? What happens in the basement?
Answer: The laundry!

GIRDLE SPELLED BACKWARDS: ELDRIG.
Oh say there Eldrig, my good man, shall we have
a spot of tea?

Dear Mrs. Plotsky:

I'm wearing your girdle now. I feel no closer
to you than before. *Au contraire.* I'd rather do a
hundred crunches a day for the rest of my life
than ever put on this instrument of the Inquisition
again. What were you thinking, making your liveli-
hood selling these to poor unsuspecting women?
What did they ever do to you to deserve such pun-
ishment? Mrs. Plotsky, you were part of the problem, not part of the solution. Shame on you.

If Mrs. Plotsky is an Enemy of the People
And I am an Enemy of the People
Am I Mrs. Plotsky?

Joseph wanted to have sex with me because of the
girdle. I looked like a different woman to him. A woman
with a different midriff, smaller waist, more waist hip
definition. Joseph was cheating on me with me. And I
let him. I am an enabler.

I was a turtle in the girdle
There was no hurdle to overcome
My mind was fertile in the girdle
An integer greater than the sum.

And unbelievably, we were already at 14th Street
and it was time to change for the Uptown Limited. After
negotiating the transfer, I lost interest in further journaling. I was so enjoying people-watching against the
backdrop of the city I loved best. People in couture,
walking at a brisk pace with great purpose, carrying

shopping bags with recognizable store names. I sat with my nose pressed to the window, fogging it up with my shallow panting, all the way to Serena's.

Her office is mid-block, in the front studio of a brownstone building on a beautiful tree-lined street not far from the restaurant *Le Refuge*. A block where the person most likely to answer the front door is a uniformed maid; where the per capita landscaping budget for seasonal plantings is a higher number than our annual vacation budget; where rose cabbages and autumnal mums now crowded every square centimeter of available soil, announcing horticulturally that this was a place of cultivation.

And so it was even more jarring than it might have been elsewhere to see streamers of yellow police tape barring entrance to her building. I stood on the sidewalk staring at the disaster, trying to make sense of the scene. The five steps that usually make up the front stoop were broken into a pile of boulders and rubble. All of the glass in the front door had been shattered, and even the iron security bars had been melted into abstract fluid shapes by whatever force and heat had blasted the doorway.

A face appeared in a wide crack between the boards securing the front window.

"Serena, what on earth?"

"Enter through the cellar, Frances. I'll meet you with a flashlight and bring you up."

"Are you sure? Is it safe?"

"We can talk about your fears when you get inside, Frances. The green door. Just step over the police barrier, or shimmy under it, whatever works."

In Mrs. Plotsky's girdle I wasn't doing much shimmying, so I carefully picked my way over the debris and over the tape and opened the creaking door, hardly secure on its own hinges. The banister on the staircase leading down felt none too stable and I braced myself between the walls in the dusty, dark passageway. Serena, standing at the base of the stairs, blinded me with her flashlight.

"Jesus," I cried, sure I'd be seeing spots for the next fifteen minutes.

"Sorry." She quickly righted the light beam, pointing it at the steps in front of me, instead of shining it directly into my corneas.

"What happened here?"

"Long story. Take my hand and watch your head. Low beam coming up."

"It's like we're in an exploded mineshaft, Serena."

"That's what everybody says. C'mon. Just a few more steps." Silt fell from the ceiling. "Some settling," she explained.

Incredibly, in the kerosene lantern light she was using for illumination, I could see that her office was pretty much the same. A small crack was visible in the statuette of Freud's bust displayed on the mantle piece, and fine gray dust coated her desk, but otherwise her sancto sanctorum was intact. Serena, too, looked the same. She was wearing a pair of beige woolen slacks without a mark on them and a rosy silk blouse with a feminine tie at the collar, which perfectly matched her lip gloss. She beckoned for me to sit on the sofa as usual, as she took her place in her cozy but elegant upholstered armchair.

I lowered myself with only minor impairment from the girdle onto the firm cushions.

"Are you wearing the girdle now, Frances?" Serena asked.

"Yes."

"Interesting." She made a note. "I see you also have a stye."

"Uh-huh. What happened to your building?"

"What do you imagine happened, Frances?"

"Gas explosion, disturbed patient arson, crystal meth lab blown sky high?"

"Hmm," she said, scribbling. "Nothing quite so dramatic. Did you bring the journal as I asked?"

"Yes," I said, handing it over. "That's it? You're not going to offer any explanation to these rather unusual circumstances? I'm just supposed to piece it together little by little from whatever clues I can pick up here and there and hope the ceiling doesn't fall on my head before I figure it out?"

"The sky is falling, the sky is falling," she said, chuckling to herself. "A kind of sudden erosion is how the engineer explained it." She opened the journal and read the first entry. "A children's song. Good. Tell me about the song."

"'Found a Peanut?' I don't know that there's much to say."

"The tune? How does it go?"

And I sang it to her.

"Sounds like 'Clementine.'"

"I suppose it is."

"What's 'Clementine' about?"

"The song? A miner's daughter in the Gold Rush."

"A daughter?" Serena scribbled. "What happens to her? Does she find her fortune?"

"*Hit her foot against a splinter, fell into a foaming brine,*" I sang.

"She drowns as the result of a clumsy accident?"

"Right."

"We could spend a whole session just on this." The kerosene lamp flickered and she got up to trim the wick. "The engineer's theory is that the negative energy from all of my patients' monstrous projections aimed at me over the decades collected into, and this is not a technical term, an Emotional Air Pocket, if you will."

"What? Is that even possible?"

"It's what he said. Let's see what else you've put out there. The next entry is some wordplay. I have to say, you have the most fascinating mind, Frances. Let's look closely at some of these. Dirigible. The Latin root is *dirigere*, which means to direct. A dirigible is an airship meant to be steered or controlled by others."

"I didn't know that."

"Your subconscious did. Again, we could spend an entire session parsing these words, seeing the interconnections, letting the narrative unravel. What's especially interesting is that this series ends with the word confession. Confession."

I gulped and nodded. She read on.

"In the next entry you allowed yourself to make the connection between the existence of the girdle and your own existence. 'Foundation garment from the fifties.' And we know from the prior entry that the girdle is dirty or soiled, or feels itself to be. And now you mention laundry. Coincidence? I could write a paper on this one alone."

"This building isn't actually condemned, is it Serena? Do they know we're in here? Bulldozers aren't just going to appear out of nowhere and raze us, are they?"

"No. I assure you. The Emotional Air Pocket is like a black cloud concentrated with acid rain, and finally it not only rained, it poured, and this destruction was the result. The worst is over."

"Is it fixable?"

"He's bringing in an HVAC expert, and a phenomenologist from Princeton, a former protégé of Albert Einstein, actually. They'll recalibrate the ventilator or something, and it should stabilize. Who's Eldrig to you, Frances. Who's your good man Eldrig?"

"No one. It's nonsense. It's just girdle spelled backwards."

"I understand. We'll come back to this one, if we have time. This letter to Mrs. Plotsky is an amazing document. You accuse her of being a torturer. Who else have you accused of being a torturer?"

"The so-called president."

"Right. You use the word shame. And in the very next entry you equate yourself with Mrs. Plotsky."

"It was a question."

"A question with the answer already built in. Are you Mrs. Plotsky? What are you ashamed of? And then the next entry's about sex. Sex, authenticity, identity, and enabling. This journal could be the subject of a symposium. There's so much to unearth, I don't think I could do it alone."

"Hmm," I said, sniffing.

"And you end with a poem. I was a turtle in the girdle. Let's talk turtle."

"Retractable head. Protective shell. Glacially slow pace."

"Good. You write 'There was no hurdle to overcome.' What's your biggest hurdle right now, would you say?"

"Living life finally on something resembling my own terms."

"Excellent. So why is there no hurdle in the girdle?"

"Because the girdle's so tight, it cuts off any and all possibilities," I said, squirming in my seat. "When I'm in the girdle, I've already surrendered. I might as well be prostrate. I'm vanquished in the girdle, hence no hurdles. There's no room at the inn."

"'My mind was fertile in the girdle, an integer greater than the sum,'" she read aloud. "Do you know what an integer is?"

"Yes, it's a whole number, not a fraction, or a mixed number."

"It's also a complete entity. Completely unrelated to mathematics. I'm overwhelmed by this last line. I don't even know where to start. Fortunately, I've had another cancellation and we can do a double-session."

"Gee, Serena, do you think if you found a safer place to hold therapy you might not be getting so many cancellations?"

"Why the hostility, Frances? Why the resistance, just when we're getting close to decoding why you're manifesting this whole 'Enemy-Combatant posture' and steamrolling toward detention?"

"Did you just say I'm deliberately manifesting my own detention? Don't you even know what's happening in this country? I am not that powerful, I assure you. There are forces bigger than both of us. Why have you manifested this bunker, Serena? Why am I sitting here, waiting for that crack in the ceiling to widen and be buried alive?"

"Why are you so enraged with me, Frances?"

"Because you...you...require my rage. You feed off bad feelings. I hate people like you!"

"People like me. Therapists? Is that who you hate?"

"No. I like therapists. I like therapy. It's people like you who..."

"Who what, Frances. Say it. People like me who..."

"PHONE IT IN, BABY. Phonies who phone it in. I'm overwhelmed!" I cried, mocking her. "I need a symposium. I should write a paper. I can't do it alone. It's too much. It's just too fucking much to have to listen to your bullshit. You're not going to write a paper. You're not going to hold a symposium."

"Phonies who phone it in," she repeated, her eyes closed, concentrating on my words. "People who phone it in. Who phones it in, Frances? Who's called you recently? Who?"

"No one. No one special. Telemarketers. The *Times* reporter. Maybe my mother called me too."

"From Australia?"

I nodded.

"Really. What did she want?"

"The usual. Nothing. Everything. To suck my blood. My life. My breath. To wring out my soul and throw it still dirty and dripping on the closet floor." Words, crazy mixed-up words poured out of me.

"When did she call?"

"A few days ago. It might've been the evening before I found Mrs. Plotsky dead on the laundry room floor.

What do you care?"

"May have been, or it was?"

"Yes."

"Maybe next time we meet, you'll tell me why she called, specifically, what she wanted from you that made you believe that a military detention in Cuba was some sort of solution for you."

"Fat chance."

"We'll stop now," she said, moving quickly to the door, feeling the wall for tremors.

"Good!"

I struggled to my feet and handed her the paltry $15 co-pay. She took my hand, which I let her do, because it was the only way out. She turned on the flashlight and led me safely to the sidewalk where she hailed a yellow cab for me with a sharp whistle, the kind between the fingers. I was still furious with her but couldn't help being impressed. Thankfully the cab pulled up, so the sidewalk awkwardness was minimal.

"Take care of that eye," I think I heard her say as she made her way back through the rubble.

"FDR and Grand," I told the Middle Eastern driver, buckling my safety belt and pulling it tight, not that I could feel it. "Sir, do you think we manifest our own destiny?"

"I just had a molar extracted," he answered, un-clenching his jaw as little as possible. "Cost me almost $400."

I just sat back, or arched back, tried to relax my over-exercised mind, and enjoyed the gorgeous river-side ride with the window rolled all the way down, the air blowing hard in my face. Soon, too soon, we arrived back in the land of hooded polar parkas zipped up tight in 65-degree weather.

At the building, Frieda was being helped out of a taxi. Though her injured foot was elaborately bandaged and she was hobbling on crutches, she seemed otherwise robust.

"Frieda!" I called from my cab. "Welcome home."

"Good to be back, I guess. What happened to your eye?"

"Just a stye," I answered, paying the driver and catching up with her. "I'll put another compress on it when I get upstairs. More importantly, how're you feeling?"

"Grateful to be alive, but depressed."

"Sorry. Why?"

"At my age, to reinvent myself all over again...what can I tell you? It's daunting."

I held the front door open for her, but she stopped several feet shy of the entrance.

"What am I supposed to do with all the peanuts?"

I had no answers for Frieda, or anyone else for that matter, myself included.

Back upstairs, there was no message from Hope. I fell on the bed with a groan and began the girdle-removal process, resting intermittently as needed. There seemed to be some sort of vacuum seal, caused by the suction that was making it near impossible to slide or roll it down. I slapped myself around the waistband, like you'd knock a glass jar lid against the side of the sink, trying to rearrange the way the molecules were knitted together, and I eventually got enough play to get some downward momentum going and get the miserable garment off without too much bruising. Never, never again.

I took it immediately outside and dropped it down the garbage chute. I half expected it to glom onto the side of the narrow chute and resist, but the laws of gravity prevailed over those of inertia, and down, down, down it went, with microscopic bits of me embedded in its folds.

The phone rang and I bustled in to answer it, hoping upon hope that it was Hope, but it was Joseph again.

"Hi, honey."

"Hi. Did you get a chance to look into that question I had about the historical accuracy of scepters in Imperial Rome?"

"Yes. And they had them. They're all over the images stamped on ancient coins."

"Great! Big ones?"

"Long and mighty. Are you sure I can't come to the party with you? I could be Calpurnia, wife number three."

He laughed because I am in fact his third wife. "No. One of the teachers here is already going as Calpurnia."

"The one with the car who gives you rides home?"

"Yep. How'd you know?"

"Shot in the dark."

"Darren's going as Caligula and our principal's got dibs on Cleopatra. Once I said I was going as Caesar, the idea caught on like wildfire."

"You're a leader among men. And women, too, I guess."

"You alright?"

"Preoccupied. Trying to plan what to do with poor old Mrs. Plotsky's ashes."

"Sounds like fun. Hey, there were some men here today asking questions about us."

"At your school? What questions?"

"Where we spend our summer vacations. If we belong to any groups. Those *New York Times* fact checkers are really thorough."

"You think that's who they were?"

"Sure. What else could it be?"

They're closing in fast.

"Honey, there's a chance, I'm not certain...I might not be around when you get home today."

"That's okay. I might be a little late too. Some of us are getting an early start on our costumes and going sheet shopping. Gotta run. Love you."

I hung up the phone and flopped down in my bedroom chair, trying to make heads or tails out of my current situation.

My lawyer—AWOL.

My husband—in fantasy land.

My court-ordered therapist—totally lost her shit.

My neighbor—in a heap of ashes.

My mother—a festering wound.

My eye—infected.

My so-called president—all of the above.

My choices?

I could continue to swivel in the cloud of softly textured Italian muslin, my hands folded in my lap, waiting for the inevitable knock on the door, the way Sal from Ashes to Ashes had told me the prior inhabitant of this room had waited for him, and presumably for death before him. Or maybe there was an alternative destiny out there for me to manifest?

I stood right up and ran to my chaotic front-hall closet, grabbed the Go Bag, unzipped it with one sweeping motion, and emptied its contents on the floor. I kicked Joseph's clothes back inside, and zoomed back to the bedroom to get a few more of my own things from my dresser drawers. Who knew how long I'd have to run?

I zig-zagged around the apartment, touching my possessions, saying goodbye to my home. Back in the living room, I grabbed the folder with my father's letters and threw it in the bag with my provisions, clothes, cash, and Mrs. Plotsky's ashes. I tucked her wig under my arm, congratulating myself for having had the foresight to keep it, zipped up, and hoisted the Go Bag on my shoulder, bearing its weight across my chest. I peeped out the eyehole in my front door, and saw that the hall, for the moment, was blessedly clear. Delaying no longer, I took a deep breath and propelled myself forward with a single syllable.

"Go!"

11

Writings on the Wall

*T*hree months later.

As you may already know, my wife is a very unusual item. I'm a composer, guitarist, and early childhood teacher, not a writer, but I'll do the best I can to fill in what's happened since she left. I won't dwell on the bad days and agonizing nights when I thought she was gone and feared the worst, because it was my fault for not seeing the messages she was sending me from the get-go. Messages that were necessarily oblique, but that she trusted I would understand. It was Brainert who helped me piece it all together. He's been a great pal, no, a true friend. And I am in his debt. Frances, too, when she comes home.

He's the one who picked up her trail in the first place. He got wind of reports that a mysterious woman wearing an eye patch and an expensive, but obvious, long ash-blonde wig had attended the community meeting at Full City on the very day Frances disappeared. Eyewitnesses said that although the woman never uttered a word, her presence was somehow galvanizing.

She was reported to have been carrying a large purple overnight bag, which later I realized must have been our Go Bag, and was said to be reading historical documents throughout the meeting, sighing audibly and swabbing tears away from her unpatched eye.

When questioned by Brainert later, Josh Dishkin said he'd been too busy moderating the meeting, which got out of hand right away and stayed that way, to notice specific details. Because of the shouting, and the mess from the prolonged food fight, which resulted in shattered coffee mugs, and accusations flying around the small but crowded café about who should pay for the damage, he hadn't paid the woman much attention. But he thought it could have been Frances, no reason why not.

Looking back, I suppose I was in shock, or denial, or both, because when I went to City Opera the next night, I really expected her to show up. Even in the intermission, I bought two glasses of champagne, and waited for my wife to emerge victorious from the long, winding line at the Ladies Room to toast Donizetti and our privileged life together, as we always do when we go to the opera and realize what a fine thing it is to be human and alive and heirs to a rich and transcendent tradition. But I had to set what would have been her plastic flute down on the counter untouched before returning to my seat for the second act.

I guess it was a couple of days later, when I came

home from work and saw Fritzy Mandelbaum from the Management Office escorting a bawling Ernesto out of the lobby, carrying a carton with his belongings, Puerto Rican flag and all. Ernesto was begging for another chance, but at the exit Fritzy demanded Ernesto's keys, stripped him of his walkie-talkie, opened the door, and told him never to show his face again in Cooperative Village.

Before he left the premises, Ernesto caught my eye and said, "Tell your wife I'm sorry. I didn't mean her any harm."

I'm not proud of this, but I grabbed him by the collar and furiously spit in his face, "What do you know about my wife? If you touched a hair on her head, I'll kill you with my bare hands."

Fritzy, who's a lot younger than me and built like a wrestler, pulled me off of Ernesto and said, "He means about the library card. He's sorry. What's the matter with you crazy Italians? You attack a man when he apologizes to you? What do you do when he pokes you in the eye? Kiss him?"

At that point, I still didn't know what library card he was talking about, but that piece of the puzzle got filled in after I'd posted the Missing posters. Josh Dishkin helped me make the posters with the picture of Frances from her 50th birthday party, with her staring at the candles ablaze on her cake. Strangely, though I remembered the occasion as festive, none of the pictures from that evening showed her smiling. If anything, her expression bore a blended look of panic and something else I can't quite put my finger on—maybe pride at having made it this far, to a half-century. Maybe it was all panic. I don't know any more.

Anyway, Josh strongly suggested that I not even think about taking up precious shiva-notice space at the elevators with my poster, and to find other places to hang it, but I ignored his advice and paid the price. Within a day or two, they'd all been defaced with moustaches, one eyebrow, horns, and worse, and I had to take them down and start over. But they'd been up long enough for a single courageous Cooperator, and it only takes one, to come knocking on my door—a Mr. Clayton.

He suggested that we take a walk, and I followed him across the overpass on the FDR to East River Park, where we sat in the amphitheater. He offered me a cigar, an Aurora, which was damned nice of him, and we both lit up. It was there he told me about the crap Ernesto pulled, the library-card identity theft, and the formal investigation initiated by the FBI.

"Those goose-stepping fascists," I screamed, stomping on a wooden bench. "She could be in Guantanamo right now."

"It's possible, but they would've had to act extraordinarily quickly; I think, knowing your wife even the little that I do, it's more likely that she's evading them right here in the city—gone underground."

"The subway?"

"I meant as a fugitive. A runaway. I can tell you this: when she left the library, I'm pretty sure she was going to call your lawyer. The lawyer might know more." He puffed and the long curl of fragrant smoke, caught by the prevailing air current, seemed Brooklyn-bound.

We smoked a minute or two more, shook hands, and he left me in the open air. I called Hope from a pay phone on Cherry Street.

"Joseph, where've you guys been? I've been calling and calling since I got Frances's message last week. The phone just rang and rang and the machine never came on."

"Probably tampered with. Or broken. I'll check the equipment when I get home. So you know the situation?"

"Know it? I'm on it. I just got back from D.C., where I met with a couple of well-placed law school classmates. One's high up at Justice and another's on the hill, working for Schumer. They both promised to investigate. This could be the one that cracks the Administration's rotten egg wide open. How's she doing?"

"She's gone, Hope. She hasn't been home since last Friday."

"Oh no, Joseph. Let me see what I can find out on this end. Try not to be too upset with her. I probably would never have come right out and advised it, but given the current lawless climate, the dilution of habeas corpus, the lack of presumption of innocence, the de facto reversal of the magna carta, rampant and flagrant Geneva Convention violations, secret military tribunals, intimidation of the press and defense attorneys, and the gruesome rest of it, she may very well have done the right thing—the smart thing. Let's hope she can stay a step ahead of them until I can offer her some real safety."

"How will I find her? I just want to see her and know she's all right."

"Don't even try. You don't want to inadvertently lead them to her. Just let her be out there. Have faith in her. She's a very resourceful woman, presumably with a well-stocked Go Bag. She can take care of herself."

When I got home, I checked the front closet where the Go Bag was usually kept. What a mess it was in there, but Hope was right—the Go Bag was gone.

It was shortly after that Brainert came into it.

"Joseph," he said, when he called early one Saturday morning. "I've been working on a story on 311 citizen complaint calls, and I've come across something that might be of interest to you. Can we meet?"

"Sure. Where?"

"I'd suggest Full City," he said, "but they're still closed for repairs. How about Flowers Café?"

"The old Baskin-Robbins? I'll head over."

At the café, Brainert wasted no time, handing me some papers as soon as I sat down.

"Shit, I didn't bring my reading glasses."

"Try these," he said, handing me his.

"What am I looking at?"

"It's a transcript of a 311 call. You can skip the preliminaries. I've marked the relevant passage for you."

"Hello, I'd like to report an injustice."

"Sure. A noise violation?"

"No. So far their sinister threats have come by mail. Why don't I just tell you the problem and then we can find the appropriate category."

"Okay. Shoot."

"My complaint is that I don't think the government should torture or murder people, and call it war."

"Uh-huh."

"And I'd like it to stop."

"Okay. Anything else?"

"I think meaningful reparations should be paid to everyone who's been harmed. And the big, fat checks should be accompanied by a note, hand-written on good stationery, with the, you know, eagle seal and the *E Pluribus Unum* motto."

"Can you spell that for me?"

"Sure. E-p-l-u-r-i-b-u-s-u-n-u-m. It means 'out of many, one.' I'd like the note to be a sincere apology, begging the whole world's forgiveness and signed in the name of the People of the United States."

"Hmmm. I think the Consumer Complaint module could work if you have a receipt for services rendered?"

"I've got tax returns."

"Then you're good to go."

"Interesting. But why show me?" I asked him.

"Turn the page," the reporter said. "Look where it's highlighted in yellow right after the confirmation number. Isn't that your wife's name?"

"Yes. When was this call made?"

"Day before yesterday. From a payphone out near the Gowanus Canal. I saw the Missing posters; I can smell a story here—possibly a Pulitzer. What's going on?"

And we made a deal. I'd give him what I got as I got it, and he'd keep me informed too. He could write whatever he thought best, with one important condition: that he promised to keep Frances's whereabouts a secret until either Hope arranges an amnesty or the Patriot Act is repealed, whichever comes first.

He even offered to send out some red herrings. "The shiva was a professional turning-point for me," he confessed. "Somehow, even with the best intentions, and completely unaware that I had, I'd lost my moral compass. That evening in your living room, the Cooperators handed it back to me with such passion, I expect never to lose it again. So, I'll sprinkle in a little disinformation. If she's at the Gowanus Canal, I'll write Erie. My fight too."

"Thank you." We started to shake on it, but embraced like long lost brothers.

"And there's one more thing," he said. "Have you noticed the new graffiti all over the neighborhood? It could be related."

"I don't know what you're talking about."

He pulled out his cell phone and showed me some digital images of emphatic messages written in all caps on sidewalks and storefronts.

The first one said: CALPURNIA ROCKS WHILE CAESAR SLEEPS.

"Christ. Where was this?"

"Outside the entrance to the F train, at Delancey and Essex."

"My stop. I must've walked right past it or over it. Show me the next one."

SO-CALLED PRESIDENT BUSH: IRAQ, TORTURE, ILLEGAL WIRE-TAPPING: THREE STRIKES YOU'RE OUT!

I laughed. "Any more?"

"Lots."

Once Brainert opened my eyes to her messages, I saw them everywhere, even places I knew she would never deliberately deface or permanently scar, like the walls of Seward Park High School. That's how I realized that her paint or chalk had to be water-soluble. At first

I thought she was using charcoal, but then it dawned on me—it was Mrs. Plotsky!

And irrationally, because my love for my wife is beyond the narrow constraints of logic and sense, but is a squirrelly, animal thing clawing more ferociously at my hungry heart with every passing day and lonely night, I hoped that maybe when her supply of Mrs. Plotsky, who wasn't very big to begin with, was finished, she'd come home.

So far, that's not been the case, though now that the mid-term elections are over, and some checks and balances may have been restored, she may be honing in on the idea. Some of her recent messages have been written ever so closer to home.

And tonight, as I stare down below at a desolate street scene, I can look out the kitchen window and see, shimmering in the moonlight, her latest words, written in careful strokes on the sidewalk right near the bus stop, where if it doesn't rain, they'll be tomorrow when I go to work. And I have to say, if she were here, I'd take her in my arms and tell her, "Francesca, *mi amore*, I'm so proud of you."

Because despite everything she must be enduring, the hardships and difficulty of a life lived on the cold concrete streets, she's not complaining. Her words, given shape and form by Lana Plotsky's grit, bone, and ash, adorn the earth, and are meant to inspire.

WE

WILL

NOT

COOPERATE

THE END

Acknowledgments

A big, fat *merci beaucoup* to an immeasurably generous and graceful woman who, for more than three decades, has honored me to the core with her friendship—Kathleen Paton, a potent and exacting muse and quite simply this book's *raison d'être.*

Profound gratitude for the manifold exertions of my marvelously wise teacher, Madeleine Beckman, whose indispensable engagement with the manuscript has made it finer in every way.

Gramercy to my inamorato, Joseph de Dominicis, whose unflagging support has made this period of creative flowering possible and whose critical responses lent shape and substance to the manuscript. When he laughed, I let it be. If he didn't, the silence told me all I needed to know, and I revised until he coughed up a throaty chuckle.

Playwright and novelist, Frances Madeson,
holds degrees from Washington University
in St. Louis and the Graduate School
and University Center of City University
of New York. She began her career as
a Legislative Aide in the U.S. House of
Representatives Committee on Education
and Labor in Washington, D.C., and has
worked in NYC law firms and nonprofit or-
ganizations for more than 20 years. Since
leaving full-time employment in 2004,
she has written three novels. *Cooperative
Village* is her debut book.

francesmadeson@gmail.com

CAROL
MRP/CO.

Carol Music Recording and Publishing Company

Visit our Web site: www.carolmrp.com